Jacob Was... For Mon...

Money, and the undeniable passion that flared between them. He wasn't thinking of forever. Only three nights ago, Claire had actually been relieved to learn that he didn't love her. How could so much change so quickly?

She held out her hand and hardly noticed as the jeweler slipped a ring on.

Last night, saying yes had been so easy. She loved him. He needed her. Given time, he might well come to love her, and last night, in the private darkness they'd shared, answers had formed and flowed easily.

"Do you want a larger stone?" Jacob asked.

"If the diamond was any bigger, I'd have to start working out just to lift it. It's a beautiful ring. I just…" She turned to look at him. His eyes were frowning, intent. He wasn't taking this business of getting a ring—of getting married—as lightly as it seemed.…

Dear Reader,

Welcome to Silhouette Desire, where every month you'll find six passionate, powerful and provocative romances.

October's MAN OF THE MONTH is *The Taming of Jackson Cade*, part of bestselling author BJ James' MEN OF BELLE TERRE miniseries, in which a tough horse breeder is gentled by a lovely veterinarian. *The Texan's Tiny Secret* by Peggy Moreland tells the moving story of a woman in love with the governor of Texas and afraid her scandalous past will hurt him.

The exciting series 20 AMBER COURT continues with Katherine Garbera's *Some Kind of Incredible,* in which a secretary teaches her lone-wolf boss to take a chance on love. In *Her Boss's Baby,* Cathleen Galitz's contribution to FORTUNES OF TEXAS: THE LOST HEIRS, a businessman falsely accused of a crime finds help from his faithful assistant and solace in her virginal embrace.

Jacob's Proposal, the first book in Eileen Wilks' dynamic new series, TALL, DARK & ELIGIBLE, features a marriage of convenience between a beauty and a devastatingly handsome financier known as the Iceman. And Maureen Child's popular BACHELOR BATTALION marches on with *Last Virgin in California,* an opposites-attract romance between a tough, by-the-book marine drill instructor and a free-spirited heroine.

So celebrate the arrival of autumn by indulging yourself with all six of these not-to-be-missed love stories.

Enjoy!

Joan Marlow Golan

Joan Marlow Golan
Senior Editor, Silhouette Desire

Please address questions and book requests to:
Silhouette Reader Service
U.S.: 3010 Walden Ave., P.O. Box 1325, Buffalo, NY 14269
Canadian: P.O. Box 609, Fort Erie, Ont. L2A 5X3

Jacob's Proposal
EILEEN WILKS

Published by Silhouette Books
America's Publisher of Contemporary Romance

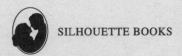 SILHOUETTE BOOKS

ISBN 0-373-76397-2

JACOB'S PROPOSAL

Copyright © 2001 by Eileen Wilks

Visit Silhouette at www.eHarlequin.com

Printed in U.S.A.

Books by Eileen Wilks

Silhouette Desire

The Loner and the Lady #1008
The Wrong Wife #1065
Cowboys Do It Best #1109
Just a Little Bit Pregnant #1134
Just a Little Bit Married? #1188
Proposition: Marriage #1239
The Pregnant Heiress #1378
*Jacob's Proposal #1397

Silhouette Intimate Moments

The Virgin and the Outlaw #857
Midnight Cinderella #921
Midnight Promises #982
Night of No Return #1028

*Tall, Dark & Eligible

EILEEN WILKS

is a fifth-generation Texan. Her great-great-grandmother came to Texas in a covered wagon shortly after the end of the Civil War—excuse us, the War Between the States. But she's not a full-blooded Texan. Right after another war, her Texan father fell for a Yankee woman. This obviously mismatched pair proceeded to travel to nine cities in three countries in the first twenty years of their marriage. For the next twenty years they stayed put, back home in Texas again—and still together.

Eileen figures her professional career matches her nomadic upbringing, since she's tried everything from drafting to a brief stint as a ranch hand—raising two children and any number of cats and dogs along the way. Not until she started writing did she "stay put," because that's when she knew she'd come home. Readers can write to her at P.O. Box 4612, Midland, TX 79704-4612.

Prologue

"We have to get married."

Outside, wind thrashed the shrubbery and snatched leaves from the oaks. Inside, three brothers stood in silence—two of them stunned, one grim. All three were tall, strong men, but that was the only obvious resemblance. They weren't full brothers, after all. A close observer might notice a certain shared grace, the identical long-fingered hands, a likeness about the jaws and strong throats. Those few people who knew the West brothers well knew of other traits their father had passed on to his sons. Less visible traits than physical strength and grace.

Less desirable ones.

Luke, the middle brother, gave a quick bark of laughter. "What, the three of us? This is Texas. I'm pretty sure there are laws against that sort of thing."

"Don't be any more of an ass than you have to." That came from Michael, the youngest, who sat in one of the wing chairs facing the empty fireplace. His eyes were as dark as his hair; he had the build of a dockworker and the face of a scholar. "The treatments are that expensive, Jacob?"

The oldest and tallest of the brothers stood in front of the mantel. Jacob West was a lean, broad-shouldered man with harsh features and a remote expression. His hair was dark enough to look black in the artificial light; his eyes were oddly pale, as nearly colorless as human irises can be. "Each treatment takes eight days and costs just under a hundred thousand dollars. None of it, of course, is covered by insurance, since it's experimental."

Michael whistled soundlessly.

"Even you don't have that kind of money." Luke pushed away from the wall he'd been leaning against. "God. The last time I saw Ada, she looked fine. It's hard to take in...how long have you known?"

"Four months."

"Four months?" Luke stopped, his head swiveling toward his brother. He was a restless man, lighter than the others in build and coloring, with the face of a fallen angel and more charm than was good for him. "Four months, and you didn't tell us?" He took a step toward Jacob. It looked as if he might take a swing at him, too.

Michael stood and put a hand on Luke's arm. "Easy."

"Ada insisted that I promise not to tell anyone. I wouldn't have known about her condition myself if I hadn't found her collapsed one day..." Jacob's thin lips closed tightly on that memory. "I'm breaking my promise now because there's something we can do."

Michael spoke. "Where's Ada now, Jacob? In the hospital?"

"No, she's in Switzerland, at the Varens Institute. They specialize in rare blood diseases. I've made copies for both of you of the information I've gathered so far about Timur's Syndrome, and about the institute.'' He passed them each a folder.

Silence fell once more while the two younger brothers looked over the multipage report. After skimming several pages, Luke grinned. ''You had her doctor investigated.''

''Of course. It's always useful to know who you are dealing with.''

Michael set the report down. ''This treatment she's undergoing is experimental. Is it safe? Is it helping?''

''At this point Ada is responding well. Well above expectations. This isn't a cure, but it looks like her symptoms can be almost completely alleviated with continued treatments. That's why I sent for you.''

''I've never used more than the interest on my coming-of-age money,'' Michael said. ''I can live well enough without it.''

''A generous offer, but it wouldn't be enough. Ada will need between two and four treatments a year for the rest of her life. The cost will come down if the treatment becomes approved in this country, but that's at least five years in the future, possibly more.''

''You're talking about between two and three million dollars over the next five years. More after that.''

''Yes.''

Silence fell once more, broken only by the limb of one young tree tapping repeatedly against the window, sounding like fretful fingers.

There was only one way they could help Ada. Marriage.

''Well.'' Luke raised his eyebrows. ''Anyone want to place a bet on which of us can do the deed first?''

Michael ignored that. ''How long will it take to wind up the trust once we've fulfilled the conditions?''

''At least a month,'' Jacob said. ''Ada will need another

treatment in three to six months. I can cover the cost myself, but I've got a deal trying to go south. If it does, it will be...expensive.''

"So we marry sooner, rather than later. No problem." The glitter in Luke's eyes contrasted with the lightness of his voice. "I can think of several ladies who would be delighted to help me out, considering how much will be left even after we take care of Ada. Jacob, of course, will ask Maggie."

Jacob's lips tightened. "Arranging my affairs for me?"

There was challenge in the look Luke gave his brother. "Don't tell me you've been leading the poor girl on."

"Are you talking about Maggie Stewart?" Michael's eyebrows lifted when Jacob nodded. "Are you serious about her, then?"

Jacob's shoulders lifted in a small shrug. "I've been considering marriage. It seemed time."

"What about you, Mick?" Luke's use of Michael's nickname was an olive branch of sorts. "You wouldn't meet many women in your line of work. Sneaking into hostile countries, blowing up things—it can't leave you much time for socializing."

"Luke has a point," Jacob said. "Will your duties interfere with finding a bride? You said you'd be leaving the country again soon."

"Yes. On the third."

Luke whistled. "Eight days? I'm a fast worker, but that's not much time, even for me. With all those millions that will land in your lap soon, though, it can be done. Want me to send a few candidates your way?"

Michael scowled. "I think I can find a wife on my own."

"One more thing," Jacob said. "The treatment seems to have worked, but there's no guarantee subsequent treatments will have the same effect." He paused. "We might marry, dissolve the trust, set up another one to pay for Ada's care—and a month or a year later, she could be dead anyway."

Luke and Michael exchanged glances. For once, the two understood each other perfectly. Michael spoke for them both when he said, "A month, a year, twenty years—it doesn't matter. Any time we can buy her will be worth the price. This is for *Ada*."

It was settled. The three of them would find women willing to marry quickly, and so dissolve the bizarre trust their father had set up. They would do this in spite of the fact that each of them had at some point vowed never to marry.

Because this was for Ada. The one woman they all loved. Their housekeeper.

One

Rain washed the window where Jacob stood staring out at a wet, dreary world. He didn't know why some people claimed to like rainy days. Rain sucked the color out of everything and sniffled in self-pity while it did, sounding like one great, endless sob. And a December rain was the worst, cold and endlessly gray.

Storms, now—storms were all right. When the air cracked open and flashed threats across the sky in million-volt arcs of light, it woke a man up. But three endless rainy days made Jacob want to put his fist through something.

Not that he would do such a thing, of course. He took a sip from the mug in his hand, then frowned. Cold coffee was as bad as rainy days.

Of course, if he wanted to be honest, he'd admit that his mood this morning had a great deal to do with what had happened last weekend. It wasn't every day a man asked a woman to marry him. And got turned down.

He'd rushed things. He knew that, but what choice had he had? He had to marry soon, and Maggie had been his choice. She was perfect for him, a warm, outgoing woman with dozens of friends both male and female, and a ruthlessly competitive streak when she was on the back of a horse. But sexually she was shy, inexperienced. He'd rather liked that about her. Jacob hadn't objected to taking his time, letting her get used to him.

Hadn't he spent two months proving she could trust him, that he wouldn't pounce on her? It hadn't been easy, either. And the reason she'd given for refusing him had come as a shock. Like hell he didn't want her! Maybe he didn't feel some blind, all-consuming passion, but she was a cute little thing and he'd been looking forward to taking her to bed. Passion was like fool's gold, anyway—lots of sparkle, no substance. He'd expected her to agree with him about that.

Of course, Maggie had been shocked, too. But she liked him, dammit. They could have been good for each other, comfortable together. If he'd just had a little more time…

When the door behind him opened, he spoke without turning. "The office line rang a minute ago."

"Then you should have answered it," a tart voice said. "Since you've apparently got nothing better to do."

He turned around. "I'm taking a break. You're always telling me I work too hard."

A tiny, wrinkled woman in baggy slacks came into the room bearing an insulated carafe of coffee—no doubt her excuse for barging in on him. "There's a difference between taking a break and brooding."

"I don't brood."

It had been three weeks since Ada had returned from Switzerland and learned that he'd told his brothers about her condition. She had yet to forgive Jacob for spilling her secret. She was looking better, though. That was what mattered. Oh, she was still too skinny, but she had always been a bony little thing. Her movements were reassuringly brisk.

"I like the hair."

One child-size hand came up to pat the orange frizz that made such an interesting contrast with her tanned-to-leather skin. "Do you? I was afraid Marilyn used too much Tropical Sunrise this time."

"Very cheerful."

She snorted and set the carafe down on his desk. "As if you cared about cheerful. You want me to call a temp agency? Cosmo's down with a stomach bug, and I've got better things to do than answer your office line."

Damn. "My new assistant should be capable of answering the phone. *If* she ever gets here."

"She called. She's on her way."

He glanced out the window. This damned rain! "I suppose the roads are difficult." Although Jacob's house was built on high land, several of the roads nearby flooded when they had a heavy rain. That was one reason he preferred to have his staff live in.

"They've got travelers' advisories out. Here." She held out a fresh cup of coffee. "Maybe a little caffeine will stop your snarling."

Jacob took the mug. He wasn't looking forward to breaking in a new assistant. He'd always hated having strangers around him. Sonia, his regular assistant, thought highly of Ms. McGuire, but Jacob remained skeptical. "I know her name from somewhere."

Ada gave him a pitying look. "They do say the brain is the first to go. She compiled a report for Sonia a month ago. You read the report. No doubt her name was on it."

"That's not what I meant." He sipped the coffee and sat down behind his desk. "It sounds like I've got time to put a call through to Marcos in Rome. When my new assistant finally shows up, bring her to me right away. You can fill her in on my faults later.''

"Aren't enough hours in the day to do *that*,'' she said, going to the door, where she paused, looking uncharacteristically uncertain. ''Jacob...''

''Yes?''

''Did Maggie turn you down?''

He knew very well his expression hadn't given him away, but apparently something had. He nodded.

''She wasn't right for you, anyway,'' she said gruffly. ''You might as well get some work done. Better than brooding.'' She pulled the door shut behind her,

In spite of everything, he smiled. Ada was definitely feeling better.

And that, he reminded himself, was what mattered, not who he married. Marriage was an unholy risk, no matter who he asked. Maybe, he thought, sipping his coffee, he would ask his new assistant to marry him as soon as she stepped in the door. *Good morning, Ms. McGuire. I'm pleased to see you didn't drown on the way here. You'll need to answer the phone today, since my secretary is sick. Also, I would like to get married as soon as possible. Is Friday good for you?*

Jacob chuckled and put down his mug. He was still smiling as he powered up his computer, accessed the latest market quotes—and promptly forgot his coffee, the rain and the woman who had rejected him.

It was still raining when Claire pulled up in front of the West mansion. *Or castle,* she thought, eyeing the massive house where she would be living for the next month or more.

Someone had already decorated for Christmas, though Thanksgiving was only a few days behind them. Lights were strung in a zigzag along the pediments topping the first floor windows, making a bright, incongruous splash of scarlet against the gray stone. Off to the left, she glimpsed a turret through the blur of rain. And could the roof really be crenelated?

Good grief. Tucking her laptop beneath her raincoat and shielding herself as much as possible with her umbrella, she climbed out of her cousin's Bronco and dashed up the steps.

The doorbell was tucked inside a gargoyle's snarling mouth. She grinned and pressed it, wondering who would open the door. A house like this deserved an ancient family retainer. A terrifyingly dignified butler, maybe? Or a hunchback with a scar that knit half his face into a hideous scowl? Igor, in fact.

The door didn't creak when it opened, unfortunately. And that was definitely not Igor.

"Good God," exclaimed the wrinkled elf in the doorway. "This is worse than I'd expected. Or maybe better."

The woman was no bigger than a twelve-year-old child. A scrawny twelve-year-old. Frizzy hair the color of marigolds and the texture of a dandelion puff framed a face that had been browned by the sun of at least fifty Texas summers. She wore a sweatshirt, baggy olive-green slacks, an apron and a pair of diamond earrings with stones so big they should have come out of a Cracker Jack box.

But Claire was pretty sure they hadn't. "Ah—I'm Claire McGuire."

"Of course you are. Who else would show up in this weather, looking the way you do?" She shook her head. "You may as well come in. Sonia did warn me. She also assured me you wouldn't try to seduce the boy, but you wouldn't have to try very hard, would you?"

Claire stiffened. "I beg your pardon?"

"Never mind." The tiny woman chuckled. "Damned if I know what Sonia was thinking, but it's going to be interesting around here. Come with me."

Claire followed her into the foyer, dripping onto the creamy marble floor. She supposed a brilliant, eccentric recluse ought to have an unusual housekeeper, especially if he didn't have an Igor. "You're Ada, I take it?"

"I should have introduced myself, shouldn't I? I figured Sonia had told you about me."

"She said I would like you."

"Some people do. You don't have any luggage? Here, give me your raincoat so I can hang it up in the kitchen to dry."

Obediently Claire slipped out of the dripping coat. "I left my suitcases in the car. If it ever stops raining, I can get them then."

Ada accepted the coat. "There's a powder room under the stairs if you want to mess with your hair or face." She gave Claire another once-over, then grinned. "Not that you need it. Oh, my," she said, turning away. "It will be interesting around here."

Claire shook her head in amusement as the tiny woman trotted under an arched doorway, and off down the hall beyond.

The foyer was classical in style—square, marble and oversize, with a twelve-foot ceiling rimmed in ornate moldings. To her left was a closed door flanked by an enormous Christmas tree. A grand sweep of a staircase lay to her right, and directly in front of her were two arched doorways—the one Ada had gone through, that led to a hallway, and another that opened onto a shadowy, unlit living room.

Her hair felt flat and damp to the touch, so she pulled a brush out of her purse. She didn't bother to hunt up the powder room, though. She had her share of vanity, but she already knew what she looked like. She didn't know nearly enough about her new employer. She hadn't even met him yet.

Oh, she'd heard about him. Who in the Dallas financial community hadn't heard of the Iceman? Jacob West was said to be brilliant, reclusive and eccentric. Some disliked him, many envied him. A few feared him. All agreed on two things: he was uncannily good at making money, and he never lied. He might be secretive, he might be ruthless, but his word was more dependable than a signed contract from most men.

One of West's eccentricities was that he didn't have an office. He lived and worked here, in the huge old house his grandfather had built, and he insisted that his immediate staff live here, too. So here Claire was, for now. She was replacing her friend Sonia, who'd flown to Georgia to pamper her daughter and spoil her brand-new grandbaby for a month or two.

Normally, Claire wouldn't have accepted a job that took her away from home and the business she'd been building, not even for a chance to work with a wizard like West. After putting in her time in the investment department of a large bank, last year Claire had moved out on her own as an investment analyst, specializing in reports to and about midsize companies. She loved it. Dissecting and interpreting a dry financial report appealed to the tidy part of her nature—not surprising in a woman who organized her closet by color, style and season.

But the part of her work that excited her, the part she truly loved, was digging for the hidden gold or buried secrets that made or ruined an investment. Claire might be as tidy as a cat about some things but, like a cat, she enjoyed the hunt. And she liked to win.

So far, she'd won often enough to keep her head above

water, but building a clientele took time. The salary she would earn from Jacob West wouldn't hurt her personal financial picture, she admitted.

But that wasn't why she'd taken the job. Not the biggest reason, anyway. More important was that she would be living here. According to Sonia, the West mansion had an excellent security system.

Things weren't normal now. Not since she'd gotten Ken's letter.

Claire shivered and stuffed her brush back in her purse. To distract herself, she wandered over to the huge Christmas tree. It was impressive, a decorator's delight, covered in old-fashioned ornaments. Impressive and lovely…and rather cold, she thought.

"Sorry I took so long." Ada's voice came from the arched entry to another hallway, startling Claire. "I made the mistake of checking on Cosmo. Never was a man yet who didn't think he was dying whenever he catches some little bug."

"Cosmo—?" Claire started to ask who that was, but the little woman had already spun around.

"Come on." Ada hurried briskly down the hall without looking to see if Claire was following. "He's probably finished talking to Rome by now. And if not, he should be."

Bemused, Claire followed. The housekeeper stopped in front of the first door on the left, knocked once, then shoved it open. "She's here," Ada announced. "You owe me twenty."

Claire reminded herself that she'd been Sonia's choice for the position, and Sonia knew her background. Probably she'd told Jacob West about it…and if not, no doubt he would recognize her. A lot of people did. Even after six years, people often took one look at her and remembered the gossip, the scandal and the trial.

Taking a deep, steadying breath, Claire stepped into Jacob West's office. She had a quick, vague impression of wood—an enormous wooden desk, carved wooden wainscoting, cabinets of some kind.

Mostly, though, she noticed the man.

Power. That was her first, overwhelming impression. The physical details filtered through that aura of power. Jacob West was a hard man, dark-haired and harsh-featured, with a lean, strong body clothed in custom-tailored trousers and a crisp dress shirt. He was also tall, she realized when he stood up behind his desk. She was five foot nine, and he stood at least six inches taller.

He nodded at Claire, but spoke to his housekeeper. "The bet was for ten o'clock. It's twelve minutes after."

"She got here before ten. Pulled up in the driveway at five minutes till, but you were on the phone." She held out her hand, wiggling the fingers. "Pay up."

"Why don't we let it ride? Double or nothing that you won't follow the doctor's orders this afternoon and nap."

Ada snorted. "You won't get me that easy. Pay up."

The glimmer in those icy eyes might have been anger, or amusement, or even fondness. Impossible to tell. He pulled out a money clip and peeled off a bill. Ada took it, tucked it into her apron pocket and trotted for the door.

She paused long enough to say, "Lunch is at one. Burritos. Don't let Jacob push you around. The boy has things too much his way, too much of the time."

The door closed behind her with a firm click.

"Well." Claire couldn't keep from smiling. "Sonia told me I would like Ada. I think she was right."

The trace of emotion that had lived in his face when he spoke to his housekeeper left when she did. He looked directly at Claire.

Such odd eyes, she thought. The color of a cloudy winter

sky, neither blue nor gray, and very pale, fringed by lashes as dark as his hair. Pale, sexy, cold…at first.

It wasn't recognition she saw in his eyes. It was heat, rich and dark and starkly sexual.

He hid the reaction quickly, so she ignored it, crossing to him and holding out her hand. "I'm looking forward to working with you, Mr. West."

His hand was hard and warm and slightly callused—and heat licked up her spine, followed by the quick, sharp bite of panic. Dammit, of all the times for her hormones to kick in—! She'd handle it, she assured herself as she dropped his hand a little too quickly. She wasn't a wild kid anymore.

"Sonia speaks highly of you." His voice was as cool and contained as his expression. "I'm glad you were able to accept my offer. I intend to make the fullest use of your talents."

"Good. I hope to learn a lot from you while I'm here."

"Perhaps you will," he murmured, and moved away from the desk. "I'll put you to work as soon as possible, but you'll need to familiarize yourself with some of my projects first."

The file cabinet he went to was one of four lined up neatly against one wall. Instead of the usual gray or beige metal, though, these were made from the same rich cherry wood as his desk.

All in all, West's office was more manor house than castle or mansion, she decided. Beautiful, expensive, with a restrained elegance.

Rather like the man. Not that he was beautiful, not with those harsh features, but he did have a certain elegance. Funny. She hadn't thought power and elegance had much in common, but when she looked at him…

Sternly Claire brought her thoughts back to business.

"You want me to read up on your current projects before I tackle anything concrete?"

"Yes." He brushed aside a dangling stem and unlocked the top drawer in one cabinet.

The stem he'd pushed aside belonged to an ivy. Not any ordinary ivy, however. This one sprawled across the tops of all four file cabinets like an invading army. Having claimed its immediate territory, the plant now had designs on the floor, judging by the way tendrils snaked down here and there.

A single red Christmas ball dangled from one of those tendrils. She smiled. "Don't look now, but I think your ivy has eaten your files."

"The damned thing won't stop growing." He pulled out one file folder, closed that drawer and opened another one. "Two years ago, when Sonia gave it to me for Christmas, it was in a six-inch pot."

"Have you considered feeding it less?"

"I don't feed it. Sonia does, though I've never caught her at it. She won't let me get rid of it."

The Iceman's assistant wouldn't *let* him get rid of a plant? Claire accepted the stack of files he held out. "I think it's massing for an assault. You'd better be careful. Your desk is only a few feet away."

He smiled. And her knees went weak. "It's pretty fast as vegetation goes, but as a member in good standing of the animal kingdom, I'm faster. I think I can evade any sneak attacks."

"Yes, of course." And she was an idiot, chattering about the man's plant and trying to keep from panting. Or grabbing him. What was wrong with her? She smoothed out her expression. "If you'll show me to my office, I'll start reading."

"This way." He moved to the opposite wall, where a

door was nearly hidden in the elaborate wainscoting. "Pay particular attention to everything relating to the Stellar Security deal. I'll be needing a report on one of the participants as soon as possible."

She followed him into the adjoining office—and stopped dead.

There was a bed in the room. Well, in one section of a very long room, the half that wasn't office. There was also a television, easy chairs and other furniture, with a tiny kitchenette tucked in one corner.

The other corner held the bed.

"Unfortunately my secretary is ill," he was saying. "So— What's wrong?"

"I, ah, hadn't realized that my living quarters and my office were going to be one and the same."

"I had this room converted when Sonia's arthritis made using the stairs difficult. Is there a problem with it?"

"Oh, no. No problem. I was just surprised. It's a pleasant room, actually. In a *green* sort of way."

And it was, on both sides of the divider. The ten-by-twelve-foot office area held an L-shaped desk with the usual computer paraphernalia, a bright green swivel chair, a visitor's chair, file cabinets, a bookcase and floor-to-ceiling shelves. And what looked like a couple hundred plants.

African violets basked under a special light in the shelves; several varieties of ferns snuggled into one corner, nearly hiding the bookcase. A ficus competed with a small palm and some other tropical plant for space in front of the window, while more plants that she couldn't identify occupied every bare spot on the desk, shelves and bookcase. A relative of the ivy in West's office was trying valiantly to cover the latticed screen that separated the office section from the bed/sitting room.

Claire shook her head wonderingly. "Sonia asked me to look after her plants while I was here. She didn't mention that she lives in a jungle."

"Sonia likes plants."

"So I see. I suppose you have to count yourself lucky she's only given you one."

"I threatened to spray her room with weed killer if she did it again."

"That's a joke, right?" But there was no glimmer of amusement in those eyes...quite fascinating eyes, really, the sort that made a woman wonder what they looked like when—

"Would you mind if I called you Claire? I prefer to be on a first-name basis with my staff."

A cowardly part of her wanted to say "the more formality, the better." She suppressed it. "Of course—Jacob."

He nodded. "Ada will give you a key to the front door and explain the security system. I prefer to leave the door connecting our offices open during the workday."

She smiled. "So you can yell for me when you need me?"

"I don't yell. When you've acquainted yourself with the basics in those files, I have some letters I need to get out."

"Ah—letters?"

"You are familiar with the term?"

Her lips tightened. "I've heard of it. However, I'm an investment advisor. I prepare reports, in-depth summaries, financial evaluations. I don't do letters. Or windows. And now, I suppose, I'd better start reading."

A phone rang. There were two of them on her desk, one yellow, one green.

"The yellow phone is the office line. Answer it."

She raised her eyebrows at his tone, but went ahead and

picked up the banana-shaped receiver. "Jacob West's office. Mr. West is…" She looked a question at him.

"Unavailable. Unless it's Michael or Luke."

"…unavailable right now. If you'd like me to take a message—yes, just a moment." She took the message, hung up and swiveled. "Did you ever go to kindergarten?"

She had the pleasure of seeing him startled. "No."

"I didn't think so. The 'please and thank you' magic seems to have missed you." She held out the message. "That was Bill Prescott. He'd like you to call back as soon as possible."

"Later. I don't want to talk to anyone today, unless one of my brothers calls."

Claire had met Bill Prescott—William Prescott the Third, actually. He was the chairman of the board of a large electronics firm, among other things. He wasn't a man accustomed to being kept waiting. "Am I supposed to screen your calls, then? And handle your correspondence?"

"Until my secretary is well, yes."

"No doubt I can fit in any reports you'd like prepared in my spare time. Perhaps you want me to take dictation? Or get you a cup of coffee?"

"Do you take dictation?" he asked politely.

"It wasn't a requirement for my degree in Economics."

"Pity." He studied her a moment. "I pay my staff well. In return I expect a great deal, even from temporary employees such as yourself. If your dignity won't allow you to depart from the strict letter of your duties, tell me now so I can make other arrangements."

Tell him she wouldn't type his letters and she could go home, where she wouldn't have to compete for space with a jungle, or put up with a highhanded, irritatingly sexy man.

And wait there for Ken to show up. "I will try to be flexible."

"Good." He stopped in the doorway. "By the way, Ada supplies us with coffee, the windows are cleaned by a window-washing company and my secretary's name is Cosmo Penopolous."

"Cosmo *what?*"

"Penopolous. When he isn't suffering from a stomach virus, he's also my personal trainer and occasional sparring partner. I do expect a lot from my employees, but my expectations are based on their individual talents, not on stereotypes." He smiled that slow, killer smile. "I look forward to discovering where your particular skills lie, Ms. McGuire. And putting them to use."

Two

Claire couldn't hear Jacob's footsteps when he left. The Oriental carpet in his office was too thick. She did hear the creak of leather when he sat in his chair, followed by the quiet click of keys that indicated he was using his computer. She opened the top folder. Instead of reading the contents, though, she stared straight ahead.

He wanted to put her skills to use?

The look in his eyes…well, she wouldn't call it obvious. Jacob West was not an obvious man. But it had been personal. And sexual.

The faint tapping of keys in the other room stopped. Claire found herself listening, wondering what he was doing now. He hadn't said a word about her past. Did that mean he wasn't aware of it? Or was he possessed of an extraordinary degree of tact?

Jacob West didn't strike her as a man much interested

in tact. But he was interested in her. And she…but it was her body that was interested, not *her*. She'd get over that.

It would have been simpler if her new boss had been old or fat or interested in men, though.

She'd handle it, she assured herself. Men hated rejection. Once she'd figured that out, it had made her life a lot easier. Most men tested the waters before risking rejection with an outright pass, and she'd learned to give the right signals to discourage them. Of course, a few were so blinded by youth, hormones or sheer conceit that the only signal they would notice involved a two-by-four.

Claire didn't think Jacob West was blind. She thought he was unusually observant. That was the problem. The man made her hot, and he knew it.

This time it was his voice that distracted her. It was pitched low, as if he were talking on the phone.

I don't yell, he'd said. No, she thought, a man with a voice like that—crisp and smooth at the same time, like good whiskey—wouldn't have to raise his voice.

She huffed out an exasperated breath. Enough. West had seen her response to him, and in return he'd let her know he was interested. So, okay, that was nothing to get upset about. Eventually her lustful thoughts would die a natural death. In the meantime, she would keep them to herself.

It occurred to her that this was the man her cousin had advised her to have a screaming affair with. The thought was so absurd she chuckled. No way was she that foolish.

In the other room, he stopped speaking. Leather creaked, and she pictured him shifting in his chair, maybe stretching out those long legs of his, the thigh muscles taut beneath the pressed slacks…

There was a radio on her desk next to the yellow phone. Claire punched the power button, and some country singer started crooning about a fool-hearted man.

She listened for a moment, but couldn't hear anything from the other room over the music. Satisfied, she leaned back in her own chair and started reading.

From his office, Jacob heard the radio come on and scowled. He had five things he needed to do right now, and another ten that should be handled promptly. And all he could think about was the woman in the room next to his.

What in the hell had Sonia been thinking of?

Claire McGuire. He'd thought the name sounded familiar, but he hadn't made the connection. Not until he saw her.

He reached for the coffee he'd forgotten an hour ago. It was, of course, cold. Frustrated, he saved the data he'd been unable to concentrate on and leaned back in his chair.

Claire McGuire. The woman who had driven Ken Lawrence mad.

That was nonsense, of course. A sane man didn't lose his grip on reality because of a woman. But the phrase had made a great sound bite, and the media had played up the femme fatale angle. They'd had help with that from Ken Lawrence's parents, who had made Claire sound like a woman who could teach "fast" to a rabbit.

The Lawrences moved in the same circles Jacob did. He knew them socially, but they didn't interest him. They were snobs—dull people who made up for what they lacked in imagination by owning the right things and knowing the right people.

Six years ago when the story broke, he'd felt sorry for the parents, contempt for the son and very little interest in the whole sordid story.

Yet he'd remembered her face, had known who she was within seconds of seeing her. No surprise there, he thought, opening his address book. That face was, quite simply, unforgettable. Add to that a body made for sin, and you had a combination that could make any man beg.

Almost any man, he amended mentally as he picked up the phone.

He punched in a number he used frequently in the course of business, but his mind wasn't on what he did. Instead he saw a smooth curve of cheek and a full, unsubtle mouth. Eyes bright as the summer sky after a storm. The flare of a hip against pleated linen slacks, and a narrow waist mostly hidden by a blazer the color of those eyes.

She was nothing like Maggie. Maggie had suited him, made him relax. Claire McGuire was anything but relaxing.

"North Investigations," a pleasant voice said into his ear.

"This is Jacob West. I need to speak to Adam North."

"Just a moment, sir. He's on another line."

Jacob waited. And he saw, again, Claire's smile. It was crooked, disturbing the symmetry of that perfect face and making her seem more human. Dangerously so. And he remembered the thought that had hit him the second he saw her, before he recognized her—before, even, the impact of her beauty had time to register.

Mine.

On her fifth morning at the West mansion, Claire awoke with her pulse throbbing between her legs and dreams sleeting off her, brightly colored images slipping away with each sleepy blink of her eyes.

Erotic images. Though she couldn't remember the content of the dream, she knew it had been highly erotic. And she knew who had starred in it. *Good grief.* She stared up at the ceiling, throbbing and restless. *Is this what men have to put up with every morning?*

More to the point, was this what she would have to put up with every morning she stayed in this house?

Her real problem wasn't her boss. Jacob had behaved himself. Oh, she'd caught him watching her sometimes. And sometimes, his pale eyes went from ice to white-hot for a second, before he realized he'd been spotted and promptly slammed the shutters closed again. But he never said or did anything objectionable. Aside from the occasional display of a sneaky sense of humor that a less observant woman might have missed altogether, Jacob had been a model of businesslike behavior—demanding, yes, but respectful. Distant, for the most part. Though he had begun to seem cautiously friendly the past couple of days…

She was vastly relieved that he'd picked up on her hands-off signals. And vastly aggravated, because relief wasn't all she felt.

It was her own unruly imagination she had to watch out for. No surprise there, she thought, and grimaced. At least, it shouldn't be. Hadn't she always been the cause of her troubles? Her impulses, her lack of judgment, had snarled up more than just her own life.

Well, she wasn't going to give in to any impulses with Jacob West. She was doing her damnedest not to *have* any impulses, but she couldn't control her sneaky, hormone-prompted unconscious when she was asleep. Claire sighed and squinted at the clock. Time to get up. At least today was Friday. She could pick up Sheba this evening.

Claire was looking forward to having her cat with her again. She hummed as she popped under the shower—leaving the water cooler than usual, to discourage those wayward hormones and flush out the lingering traces of her dream.

Right now, her cat was at home with her cousin Danny, who was house-sitting. Sheba was a cat with attitude. She also possessed a worse set of impulses than Claire owned. The two traits had resulted in a serious disagreement with a neighbor's German shepherd the day before Claire started working for Jacob, followed by a quick trip to the vet. The vet had stitched up Sheba and kept her a few days, but she was doing fine now.

Clean, dry, with her hair and makeup done, Claire stood in front of her open closet door and tried to find something to wear. It shouldn't have been difficult. She liked clothes, and she'd brought a fair portion of her closet with her. But for some reason nothing looked right this morning.

Finally she settled on loosely shaped black slacks in a heavy silk that felt like pure sin against her skin, pairing them with a short yellow jacket. She slipped tiny gold hoops through her ears and glanced at the clock. She didn't want to be late for her date this morning. With Ada.

She smiled. Ada was quite a character. So was Cosmo, though of a different stripe. Even the maid who came three days a week to help keep this huge old house clean was out of the ordinary. Maude was a grandmother with enough college credits for two degrees, and no intention of getting a "real" job. She just wanted enough money to keep taking courses in whatever interested her.

They said you could tell a lot about people by the company they kept. Claire wasn't sure what Jacob's odd household said about him, but it sure didn't fit with his Iceman image.

Normally the inmates of the big old house fended for themselves at breakfast and on weekends, but during the week everyone gathered in the big kitchen for lunch and dinner. Often Jacob was there, sometimes not, depending on whether he was in town and remembered to stop working. Last night Ada had honored Claire with an invitation for breakfast. Blueberry pancakes. Claire's stomach rumbled, but she paused on her way out, glancing at the door that joined her office to Jacob's.

It was closed, of course. Every day when she shut off her computer she shut that door. And every morning when she opened it he was already in his office, already working. Sometimes she wondered if he slept there.

Acting on impulse, she snuck the door open and peeked inside. His office was dark, unoccupied. Of course it was. Jacob had a perfectly good bed in his bedroom on the second floor. Ada had pointed out his room when she gave Claire a tour of the house. Right now he was probably asleep in that king-size bed, stretched out beneath the silky black-and-brown comforter... Don't go there, she ordered herself, and inched the door closed once more.

She was reaching for the other door—the one to the hall—when her phone rang.

Dang it. Well, the pancakes could wait one minute, but no more. She picked up the receiver. "This is Claire."

"And this is your hardworking house-sitter with a good news, bad news report," her cousin's voice said cheerfully.

"Danny! I didn't expect to hear from you this early." She resigned herself to being a few minutes late. "Sheba's okay, isn't she?"

"Oh, she's fine. She got her medicine last night just like the vet ordered. And don't worry about me—the bleeding stopped eventually. You *are* coming to get that hell-spawned beast tonight, aren't you?"

She chuckled. "I'm looking forward to it."

"Not as much as I am," he said fervently.

"You're earning stars in your crown, as Mom used to tell us. I take it that was the good news. What's busted? Did the disposal spit up again?"

Danny paused. "A disposal, I could fix. This is a little more complicated. When I opened the door this morning to bring in the paper, there was something else on the stoop. A rose.''

Claire's pulse began pounding in her ears. "Red," she said, her voice flat. "It was red, wasn't it, Danny?"

"I'm afraid so."

A single rose. Bloodred, the petals barely unfurled. She could see it so clearly. Red for passion, Ken used to tell her. Only one rose, always just the one. Because they were meant to be one. Claire's fingers tightened on the receiver. "You didn't see him?"

"I wish I had. If I'd caught him—"

"Dammit, Danny, do *not* do anything macho and stupid!"

"Don't worry. I'll let your cop buddy know if the son of a bitch comes sneaking around. Doesn't mean I wouldn't like to catch him at it, just so we could prove he's violating parole."

The police wouldn't consider a rose evidence of anything. She bit her lip and changed the subject, trying to push the fear down, where it wouldn't show. To either of them. "Are you going to be home tonight, when I come get Sheba?"

"I've got a meeting at seven, but I'll be here after that. No more wild Friday nights for me," he said wryly.

His words warmed her. Danny just might make it work this time. She wasn't fooling herself. He had a lot of hard work ahead, and he might fail and fall many times. But this time he was attending AA meetings because he wanted to, not because he needed to please or fool someone else. Like her. Or a judge.

"How about you?" he asked. "Going to have a wild time tonight with your new boss, maybe?"

"Hardly."

"You do have that haughty, duchess tone down pat. How long has it been since you went out on a real date, Claire?"

"Come on, you know I don't have the time or energy for much of a social life. I'm trying to get my consulting business off the ground."

"Your career's an excuse. No, listen to me for a minute. You enjoy the money game, and you're good at it. But at heart, you aren't an ambitious person. You just like playing the game."

"Jut playing the game won't pay the bills," she said dryly. "And that, I do take seriously."

"You're hiding, Claire. Just look at your clothes."

She bristled. If there was one thing she knew, it was how to dress. "What's wrong with my clothes?"

"Those power suits of yours are just as much camouflage as the bag lady clothes you wore for a while."

"I realize you don't get the whole dress-for-success concept, but take my word for it. I need to look professional. Ninety-nine times out of a hundred, people do judge us on how we look."

His voice was sad. "I understand why you think that. But—oh, hell, Claire. Sometimes I miss you. The person you used to be, the cousin who laughed all the time and did crazy stuff just for the hell of it. The one who didn't plan her life on a blasted spreadsheet."

Silence fell, trapping too much of the past between them. "That person made too many mistakes," she said at last. Danny ought to know that. One of her impulses was partly responsible for the hell he'd been living in the past few years.

"Maybe, but she was human. I'm learning a whole lot about being human and making mistakes these days. Claire…I'm glad you got out of this house, where Ken

Lawrence can't find you. Just don't keep running away from him in other ways, too.''

"Look, I've got to go. I'll see you tonight, okay?"

After she hung up, Claire took a deep, calming breath. Danny was wrong. He was one hundred percent wrong, and she was an idiot to let him upset her. She wasn't running away. She was running *to* something—the future she'd been building and the person she was becoming: a woman who would never make the kind of mistakes that had wrecked more lives than just her own. No, she didn't miss her old self at all.

She took another slow breath, opened the door to the hall and stepped out—right into a solid male body.

A startled shriek rose in her throat. She bit it back. Her head felt light and dizzy.

"Whoa!" Two strong hands gripped her arms, steadying her.

Not Jacob. That was her first thought, and she shook her head to rid herself of it. Not Jacob—and not Ken, either, of course. He couldn't get to her here.

This was a stranger.

"Sorry," she said. "I wasn't watching where I was going."

His hands dropped and his eyes widened. "Surely you aren't Claire McGuire."

"I hate to disagree, but I am."

"Feel free to disagree with me anytime." A smile grew in his eyes until it reached his mouth. "Especially when I say something stupid. Of course you're Claire McGuire. I'm Michael West."

"Jacob's brother?"

"Guilty."

Michael was a good-looking man, but his features were even, not harsh, and rather Latin. His eyes were as dark as

Jacob's were pale—no resemblance there. His body, now…yes, physically he had something in common with his brother. Power. And control. "So you're one of the two people Jacob was willing to talk to on my first day. Glad to meet you, Mr. West."

"Make it Michael, please. Or Mick. That way I won't have to call you Ms. McGuire. Has Jacob been difficult?"

"It varies. On a scale of teddy bear to grizzly, he usually hits somewhere between rattlesnake and wolverine."

Amusement deepened in his eyes. "Sounds as if you're getting to know him quickly. Are you on your way to breakfast?"

"Yes, Ada asked me to join her. And you?" She shouldn't pump him for information about his brother, but if he happened to volunteer something…

"Unfortunately I've already eaten. I've got a ten o'clock flight."

"Oh." Looked like her curiosity was doomed to disappointment. "Well, it was nice meeting you." She smiled. "I almost said 'running into you,' but that's precisely what I did do, isn't it?"

"I didn't mind that part."

She chuckled. "I'll bet you were a hell-raiser as a kid."

"As a matter of fact, I was. I didn't think I gave that impression these days, though."

"Oh, you don't. But it takes one to know one."

He lifted his eyebrow. With that subtle shift, the resemblance she hadn't seen before snapped into focus, and he looked very much like his brother. "Are you a hell-raiser?"

"Not anymore, but when I was younger—well, who has any sense at eighteen? You remind me of my 'making up for it' period, when I was terribly serious about everything."

He studied her so gravely that she wondered if she'd

offended him. "You know, I think I do have time for a quick cup of coffee before I leave. If you wouldn't mind some company—?"

"I'd love it." She started down the hall with him, slanting him a mischievous glance. "I'll bet Ada knows all sorts of stories about you and Jacob when you were boys."

"Just don't mention the apple pie incident. Or anything from when I was a teenager. Or—hmm. Maybe it would be better if I left without a last cup of coffee, after all."

She laughed. "I think I'm going to like you, Michael. And there is no way I'll let you duck out of that cup of coffee now." Claire thrust aside all thought of the rose that had been left on her doorstep. She was safe for the moment. Ken had no way of finding her here.

And if her haven was only temporary, then, like Scarlet, she'd worry about it tomorrow. Because there wasn't a damned thing she could do about it today.

The kitchen was Michael's favorite room, maybe because it had changed so little over the years. The window box in the corner, with its crop of herbs adding a sweet whiff of oregano and mint to the air, was a recent addition. Sonia's doing, most likely. Michael sipped his coffee and enjoyed the steam and the mingling of scents. It always smelled good here.

None of his father's wives had been allowed to tamper with Ada's domain. That window box was the only tangible evidence that any woman other than Ada had ever lived in this house...that, and the woman who sat next to Ada at the big, scarred table.

Claire McGuire was a surprise. Especially after the talk he'd had with his brother last night.

Michael enjoyed watching her. What man wouldn't? But her beauty wasn't as interesting as the way she obviously enjoyed Ada, who was taking shameless advantage of the opportunity to embarrass Michael.

When Ada finished her latest story, Claire's smile broke into a laugh. "He didn't. Really? A smoke bomb?" She shook her head. "Michael, you're worse than I was. At least I never blew anything up."

"Can I help it if I like things that go boom?"

Ada shot him a darkling look. She didn't approve of Michael's frequent, lengthy absences. "The boy always did like making a commotion. *That* hasn't changed."

"Sounds like you had your hands full when they were younger."

"Hellions, all three of them," Ada said proudly. "Now, Jacob has always been sneakier about it than the other two, but he got into his share of trouble. There was this girl he was crazy about when he was fourteen. She was sixteen, so he—"

"Not the one about my first driving experience," Jacob said dryly from the doorway. "Please."

"It's your turn," Michael said. "Claire has already heard about the smoke bomb I set off at St. Vincent's."

"I'm the eldest. I should go last." He poured a cup of coffee, turned and leaned against the counter. "I vote that we tell her about Luke's gambling career next."

Claire hadn't precisely stiffened when Jacob entered the room. It was more subtle than that—a loss of ease, as if she were suddenly conscious of her expression, her body, in a way she hadn't been before. As if she were intensely conscious of Jacob's presence.

Interesting, Michael thought.

"Luke is your other brother, right?" she asked Jacob.

He nodded. He looked entirely at ease, but Michael knew better. The hunter had his prey in sight, and didn't want to spook it. "Technically," Michael said, "if we go by years rather than maturity level, Luke is my older brother. Not as ancient as the graybeard leering at you now, but—''

"Watch it," Jacob said lazily. "I can still take you, as long as you don't try any of those sudden-death tricks the army taught you."

"Not in my kitchen, you can't." Ada pushed her chair back and stood. "Jacob, you sit down instead of perching there like a vulture checking out the remains, and I'll fix you some pancakes."

A phone rang. Not the one in the kitchen, but nearby.

"That's your line, Ada," Jacob said helpfully, sipping his coffee.

"Don't you think I know that? But since I'm busy and you're not, you might offer to get it for me."

"I'd rather stay here and leer at Ms. McGuire."

Ada smirked at him. "I guess you would." She turned and trotted for the hall door, calling over her shoulder, "Claire, you keep these boys from tearing up my kitchen while I'm gone."

"I hope the two of you aren't feeling violent this morning," Claire said as Ada vanished down the hall. "I'd hate to let Ada down."

"I'm a gentle soul," Michael assured her. "Unlike my rowdy brother."

Jacob raised one eyebrow in that cool, mocking way that used to make Michael want to smash him when he was a teenager. Of course, he'd wanted to smash a lot of things back then.

Claire was amused. "Yes, I can see how rowdy Jacob is. A real troublemaker. You're in the army, Michael?"

"Special Forces. My brothers treat me with much more respect now that I know how to kill a man in thirteen seconds."

Her eyebrows went up. "At least I can tell when you're joking. I think."

"Jacob was born with a poker face. When the doctor slapped his bottom, he didn't cry—he slapped him back. Then he bought the man's practice."

"It was my first buyout," Jacob said seriously. "The man had excellent labor relations, but he'd dabbled too heavily in futures."

"That," Claire said, her lips twitching, "was a joke. A bad one, but definitely a joke."

Jacob continued to lean against the counter, sipping his coffee and talking casually with his new employee. He didn't fool Michael for one minute. Jacob had always gone after what he wanted with the single-minded focus of a lion stalking a gazelle—no nerves, no mercy and the great patience that is possible only in the absence of doubt. His big brother wasn't so much unaware of the chance of failure as he was impervious to it. A lion whose prey escaped didn't slink off and moan about his failure, or decide he wasn't really cut out for this hunting business. He went out and found another gazelle.

But had Jacob ever gone on the hunt for a woman—one particular woman? Michael didn't think so. Maggie had been—well, handy. Not prey.

"If you have any brothers," Jacob was saying, "you'll know you can't believe half of what Michael tells you about me."

"No brothers or sisters, I'm afraid, though I do have a cousin I'm close to." Her eyes softened with memory and affection. "We were hell-raisers together, way back when."

"Were you?" Jacob set his coffee cup down. "I have trouble picturing you raising hell. Raising temperatures, yes.'' He smiled slowly, all sorts of suggestions in his eyes. ''That, you do very well.''

Her eyebrows lifted in a wonderfully haughty way. ''If that's supposed to be a compliment, please don't bother.''

''A statement of fact, rather.'' He straightened, moving away from the counter. ''It's not eight o'clock yet.''

She glanced at her watch—a pretty, but inexpensive piece, Michael noted. ''If you'd like me to get to the office early—''

''No. I was pointing out that we aren't on the clock yet. If we were, it would be inappropriate for me to tell you how desirable I find you.''

''You're out of line.''

''Even in these days of political correctness,'' Jacob said, ''surely a man can indicate his interest in a beautiful woman, as long as he's willing to accept a refusal. You don't look like a woman who would have trouble saying no…if that's what you want to say.''

There was a tiny crease between Claire's eyebrows. ''I'm not. And 'no' is definitely the answer.''

She didn't look as if she believed it would be that simple. Michael knew it wouldn't. He pushed his chair back, letting it scrape loudly enough to interrupt the staring match the other two were engaged in. ''I'd better be going if I don't want to risk a speeding ticket. Walk with me to my car, Jacob?''

Jacob's eyes met his. For a moment, Michael thought his big brother would refuse—and he knew why. He grinned.

Jacob sighed. ''All right. At least the damned rain has stopped.''

Three

Jacob was in no mood for an interrogation. He would have made some excuse to avoid walking Michael to his car if he'd thought he could get away with it, but he knew his brother. Once the light of curiosity was fixed in Michael's eyes, there was no turning him aside. That curiosity had nearly gotten him killed more than once, a fact that troubled Jacob a good deal more than it did Michael.

He was more or less resigned to his fate when he opened the kitchen door and stepped out into a damp, sunny morning. After a couple of blessedly dry days, it had showered again last night.

Their grandfather had built his mansion with his gaze fixed firmly on the past, setting the garage behind the house like a carriage house from the last century. A gravel path led the way through the boxwood and yew border that screened the building from view.

"How's your head this morning?" Jacob asked.

"As unhappy as my stomach."

"If you'd drink something other than that rotgut you were guzzling, you might not have a hangover."

"But I have such a delicate constitution."

Amusement lightened Jacob's mood. "Mighty gentle flowers they grow in Special Forces."

Michael grinned, but didn't reply. Their feet crunched on the gravel. Water dripped silently from trees to bushes to ground, the drops gemmed by sunshine, and the sky was a bold, clear blue—the color of childhood, to Jacob. Of solitude and freedom.

When Michael spoke again, his voice was carefully casual. "You'll get my prenuptial agreement tucked away safely?"

When Michael had turned up unexpectedly last night, he'd announced that he was getting married and getting drunk—not in that order. The marriage would take place as soon as he got back from his current assignment.

"I'll take care of it. I wish you'd reconsider, though. I'm not looking forward to having a piranha for a sister-in-law."

Michael shrugged. "You won't have to put up with her long. There are a few things you forgot to mention last night, weren't there?"

"As I recall, we spoke mostly of your unwanted bride."

"We talked about marriage. The one I'm planning, and the delay with yours, now that Maggie turned you down. You didn't mention that you've already got her replacement picked out and under siege."

"We don't have time to be choosy." It was an accurate statement as far as it went, but he was grimly certain Michael wouldn't be satisfied with it. His youngest brother could be damnably perceptive at times.

"You've always been choosy. Take your new assistant—

a very choice specimen. In fact, she may be the most beautiful woman I've ever seen."

"Beauty is a subjective judgment, though, isn't it?"

"I suppose a male kangaroo or orangutan might not find Claire beautiful. But a man would. Any man. No doubt the man she's living with thinks she's incredibly beautiful."

Jacob stopped. "She's not living with a man."

"Did she tell you that?" Michael shook his head. "I didn't think a cynic like you would accept a woman at her word."

"I know damned well she isn't living with anyone. Adam North handled the background check himself. He's thorough."

Michael stared at him a moment, then started to laugh. "You had your prospective bride investigated?"

"Of course."

"Of course," Michael said, lightly mocking. "'All policy is allowed in war and love,' I suppose. Which are you embarked on, Jacob—love or war?"

"Business. That sounded suspiciously like poetry."

"Some eighteenth-century playwright, I think. Sorry. St. Vincent's influence lingers like cheap perfume. Tell me, did you have him run a background check when you hired her, or after you decided to have her?"

"I prefer to have as many facts as possible before entering into any agreement. Marriage is as potentially treacherous as any other partnership, and I don't know Claire as well as I knew Maggie."

"True. Which makes me wonder…you seem to have given up on getting Maggie to marry you pretty easily."

"I haven't abandoned my goal. I've simply changed one element."

"The identity of the bride, you mean?"

This conversation was beginning to irritate Jacob. "What made you think someone was living with Claire?"

"Shameless eavesdropping. Her door was open when I came down the hall, and I caught the last part of a conversation she was having with someone named Danny. I didn't catch a last name." He paused. "From things she said about some repairs, it was obvious he's living in her house. Or else she's been living in his."

Jacob's mind sorted through the data in the report he'd been reading when Michael arrived last night. "Danny is her cousin. They're close. He probably needed a place to stay, since he's out of work more often than he's employed." Was Danny important to her? It seemed likely. Jacob considered what that might mean to his plans. The way to succeed in any deal was to learn what the other person wanted badly enough to give up what you wanted in return.

"Sometimes cousins are *too* close."

Jacob's mouth crooked up. "Who's being cynical now?"

"Cynicism is one legacy from our father we don't have to wait to claim."

Memories of Randolph West always conjured mixed feelings. "True. I still hope to avoid part of his legacy, however."

Michael grimaced. "Yeah. Which is why I wasn't surprised you picked Maggie. You aren't as resistant to the married state as Luke and me, and Maggie is pretty much the type you would settle on. She's not the sort to tie a man into knots. Claire McGuire, though, surprises the hell out of me."

"You don't think I'm as susceptible to beauty as the next man?"

"Her looks are more complication than explanation. Why her, Jacob?"

Why, indeed?

She was kind. He hadn't expected that. It was the sort of kindness that rose naturally from a warm heart, brimming over onto those around her, charming without the intention to charm. Cosmo had been won over within moments of meeting her, not because she was beautiful—that could have caused all sorts of problems—but because she simply, sincerely, liked him. Accepted him, tattoos, prison record and all.

She liked and enjoyed Ada, too. What was more, Ada liked her, and Ada was a harder nut to crack than Cosmo. And she smiled at Jacob's jokes. That could have been courtesy or tact, but most people didn't even know when he was joking. She did.

Was that why he wanted her? Because she was kind, and laughed at his jokes? Banal, but true—yet not the whole truth. The moment he'd seen Claire, he'd known he would do everything he could to make her his.

He had no idea why. Jacob started walking again. "Why not her? Come on. You don't want to miss your plane."

The garage was a large brick building that smelled pleasantly of metal, oil and gasoline. Jacob had expanded it after their father died. He'd wanted to have spaces for his brothers' vehicles when they visited, because this was their home, too. There were four cars housed there now—three of Jacob's, plus Michael's aging Jaguar. Jacob had rebuilt the engine, then given him the car when he turned seventeen, a combination birthday present and bribe for sticking it out for the six months at the military academy where he'd been banished.

After that first six months, no bribes had been necessary. Michael had shocked everyone by thriving on the life.

"The Jag running okay?" Jacob asked.

"Purrs like a kitten." Michael opened the door.

"I don't suppose you can tell me where you're going this time."

"Afraid not. You've got the number to call in case of emergency."

"Yes."

Michael settled into the low-slung car, then paused, looking up at Jacob. "Did you notice that watch she has on?"

He frowned. "Claire's watch? What about it?"

"Why isn't it a Rolex? Or something with diamonds that costs as much as my car? A woman like her could have diamonds if she wanted them."

"Our experiences to the contrary, not all women can be bought. At least, not with money." He had some ideas about what Claire wanted. Tonight he'd find out if those ideas were accurate. "You'd better go before you miss your plane."

"I suppose so." He started the car.

"Michael." A familiar mix of anxiety and frustration clutched at Jacob. He couldn't keep his brother from doing what he needed to do. He wouldn't try. But it was always hard to let him go off and risk himself. "Be careful, will you?"

"I will if you will."

"I'm always careful."

Michael grinned. "The funny thing is, you probably believe that."

"I understand you met Sonia at Helping Hands." Ada plunged a frying pan into soapy water.

"Yes, we both volunteer there." Claire tied the apron around her waist. This was the first time Ada had taken her up on her usual offer to help with the dishes. She had a feeling the tart, tiny woman had something she wanted to discuss. "Sonia's one of the reasons I started my own consulting business, actually. She kept urging me to try it. Finally I did.''

''Hmm.'' Ada scrubbed the pot firmly. ''Guess her contacts haven't hurt you any.''

''I wouldn't have done as well as I have without her. She's steered several clients my way.''

''You worked with her long at that Helping Hands place?''

''About three years. She was my trainer on the hot line.'' Claire accepted the pan from her interrogator and started drying it.

''Funny that she didn't tell you about Cosmo. She never said much to me about you, either.''

''Sonia's always claimed she's allergic to gossip. We usually talk about business matters in general, her daughter, or what she thinks I should be doing with my life.'' Claire smiled, remembering the gentle, ceaseless nagging she'd received to quit her job at the bank. ''And about Helping Hands, of course.''

''Don't think I could handle that hot line stuff,'' Ada said, handing her another pan. ''I'd give the wrong kind of advice. If you ask me, anyone who likes to beat up on his wife and kids ought to be taken out and shot.''

''Sometimes I feel that way, too. But violence doesn't solve the problem.''

''It's damned tempting, though. If someone had taken a gun to Jacob's grandfather, a lot of lives would have been different. Better. Here, go wipe off the table while I get the dishwasher going. We're done with the pans.''

Claire took the sponge Ada held out, but she didn't move, shocked as much by the fact of Ada's revelation as by its implications. Though Ada had been free with stories about ''the boys,'' she'd never revealed anything truly personal. ''Jacob's grandfather beat him?''

"Not *him*. If the old man had touched one hair of Jacob's head, Randolph West would have killed him. And he made sure his father knew it." Ada nodded firmly. "The old man died just after Luke was born, so the younger boys were never in any danger. But there was no one around to protect Randolph when he was little. To the day he died, he had scars from a whipping he got when he was ten. He'd swiped a cookie."

Claire shook her head. "I've heard plenty of stories like that since I started working the hot line, but it still gets me in the pit of the stomach when I hear a new one. I can't get used to it."

"You aren't supposed to. You going to clean the table or not?"

Obediently Claire turned away to do as she'd been bidden. "I'm wondering why you told me all that."

Ada chuckled. "Don't pretend you haven't been trying to pump me for information about Jacob all week."

"I've tried," she admitted dryly. "And you've dodged every personal question I've snuck into the conversation. Until now."

"So maybe I changed my mind. He seems to like you." She tilted her head, narrowing her eyes. "Jacob's a good man, strong and honorable. But he isn't an easy man, not to know or to live with."

"I'm curious about him because he's my employer," Claire said firmly. "And, I suppose, because I'm nosy. And that's all."

Ada's expression was more of a smirk than a smile. "Of course. I just wanted you to understand. Randolph had his problems as a father—one of them being that every one of the West males could teach stubborn to a mule. But he loved his boys. When Jacob tells you about his childhood, you need to remember that."

"Jacob doesn't talk about his childhood," Claire protested. "We don't have that kind of relationship."

She snorted. "He's telling you all the time. You just aren't listening right."

Claire couldn't imagine Jacob West opening up to anyone about the trials and traumas of his childhood. Oh, she knew what Ada meant—that he revealed himself in other ways. And he did, but the glimpses she'd had of her enigmatic boss the past few days seemed to add up to several different men. Who was Jacob West, really? The casually friendly man she'd seen at breakfast? The predator she thought she saw sometimes? The cool, emotionless businessman the world believed him to be? Or the difficult, wounded man Ada had hinted at?

Damn him, anyway, for being so mysterious, she thought as she snatched a bite from a turkey sandwich between phone calls. She didn't need a brilliant, inscrutable man in her life. Not as a boss, and certainly not as anything else. Even if she did get a hormonal buzz from being in the same room with him.

Especially because of that.

Oh, but he was exactly the sort of man she'd have tumbled for in her wild and woolly days. Back then, she'd have fallen into his arms and into his bed, laughing at the thrill of it, and never doubted her ability to take care of herself and her heart. She knew better now. But for the first time in years, it was hard to ignore her unruly instincts.

It didn't help that she liked the blasted man.

Fortunately she had plenty to keep her mind occupied. Her boss had dropped yet another thick folder on her desk that morning—an in-depth financial report on a key investor in the Stellar Security takeover. "I want to know where his money is," he'd said. "And if there's any missing."

This was the sort of work Claire loved—economic detective work. It appealed to the hunter in her, and to the tidy woman who arranged the clothes in her closet by color, season and style. She was between phone calls, mainlining calories in the form of chocolate kisses while she tracked down a discrepancy in Murchison's financial statement, when a freight train rumbled up to her desk. And spoke.

"Refined sugar is bad for you," said a deep, deep bass voice. "Poisons the body, weakens the immune system."

She looked up and smiled. "I won't ask if you want a kiss, then."

Cosmo Penopolous was her height and roughly three times as broad, and every bit of that breadth was muscle. He had Groucho Marx eyebrows, a bandit's mustache and a fondness for jewelry that could be implanted in his body. Both ears were double-pierced; there was a gold ring in his nose, and another in his left eyebrow. A tattoo crawled up one thick forearm.

And he blushed. Easily. Color flooded his face now, darkening his already swarthy complexion. "I didn't mean…we have to live in our bodies, right? It makes sense to keep them strong and healthy."

She'd figured out within minutes of meeting Cosmo that he was religious about fitness and nutrition. Instead of fielding passes, she'd had to field offers to help her build muscle tone. "I'm sure that's true."

"So when are you going to let me get you started on some weight training? Jacob won't mind if we use the gym. The boss man likes to have it to himself between six and seven in the morning, but any other time is fine. Just let me know."

"I don't think weight training is for me," she said apologetically. "I don't really want to bulk up."

"You don't have to. That's the beauty of it. You can

add bulk or slim down, get stronger, build endurance—whatever you want. Depends on how you do it." He beamed at her, happy as a missionary with a possible convert. "Here, I'll show you."

Ten minutes later, he was sitting on her desk after showing her the proper way to do bicep curls, using her stapler in lieu of a weight. "I'm not certified, but I'm working on it. This, see, it's my passion—making the most of our bodies. Everyone should have a passion, right?"

She cocked her head curiously. "How did you end up a secretary if your real love is fitness?"

"I like secretarial work, too. It's…neat. I like things neat." He cleared his throat self-consciously. "Didn't always. I took some wrong turns, but that's how we learn, right? Screw up often enough and you either get smart, or you get dead. Me, I got to where I liked things orderly." His sudden grin looked ferocious beneath that mustache. "Learned how to type, too."

Cosmo had learned how to type while doing three-to-five for grand theft, she'd learned on her second day here. "And came to work for Jacob."

He leaned forward. "I owe him a lot. Gonna owe him even more when I open my gym, but that's money. That I can pay back. I'm not ready to go into business yet, but in a year or so, you'll see. Jacob said—"

"Taking my name in vain, Cosmo?"

Jacob stood in the doorway, all cool control, one eyebrow lifted. A prickle of awareness danced over her skin, and heat swam like sunshine in her blood.

Why did this have to happen to her now?

Cosmo made a low, rumbling noise—his laugh. "I may curse you sometimes, boss man, but I don't curse by you. You need something?"

"I need that contract out by five today, but you already knew that."

"It'll be ready. Even us grunts are allowed a lunch break."

"Lunch, yes. Flirting, however, must be done on your own time." He turned to Claire. "I need you to go with me to a party tonight."

Her eyebrows went up. "I beg your pardon?"

"It's business," he said impatiently. "Murchison is determined to start the round of holiday parties early, and I need to be there. He's been making noises about pulling out of the Stellar deal."

"Ouch." Murchison was the man whose money she'd been tracking all morning. The takeover might be in trouble if he pulled out. "Still, I don't see why you need me."

"Because Sonia isn't here. I need an extra set of eyes and ears, preferably guided by an intelligent mind. The party will be cocktails followed by a late, buffet-style dinner. Do you have something to wear? Sonia was supposed to tell you to bring some dressy things."

She had. But Claire did not want to play dress-up with this man. She especially didn't want to go to any party where she might run into people who had known her as Ken Lawrence's fiancée. "I have plans for tonight. If all you need is a second set of ears, take Cosmo."

Cosmo shook his head sadly. "No, those folks wouldn't be comfortable with me. You go, Claire. It will be good for you." He stood and shook his finger at her. "But stay away from the refined sugar, hear? I'd better get to work before the boss man accuses me of flirting again."

As soon as Cosmo left, she looked at Jacob, amused. "Your secretary is a tattooed ex-con. That's even better than an Igor."

"What?"

"Never mind. About tonight—"

"Be ready at seven. Murchison's place is outside of town."

"I told you, I have plans." In the past four days, she'd seen no sign that he was aware of her past. If she went to the Murchison party with him, she would have to let him know about Ken and the scandal. And she didn't want to.

"A date you can't break?"

"Yes. With my cat."

He looked blank. "Your cat?"

"She's been at the vet's—a little disagreement with the neighbor's dog. I'm supposed to pick her up tonight." She stood. "Sonia said I could bring Sheba with me. If that's a problem, I'll help you find someone else for the position."

His eyebrows lifted. "You'd rather quit than be parted from your cat for a month?"

"Absolutely." Claire wasn't bluffing. God only knew where she would go if she didn't stay here, but she had no intention of letting Sheba think she'd been abandoned. She wasn't sure she ought to stay here, anyway. In his house. Fighting the urge to reach up and test the texture of the skin drawn tight over his lean cheeks.

His mouth kicked up at one corner. "Fine. We'll pick up your cat after the party. I hadn't planned on staying late."

"I live in Garland. It's out of your way..." She frowned. "Why do you look so pleased?"

"Some surprises are pleasant." His eyelids drifted lower, and a slow smile filled those pale eyes. It was as intimate in its way, that smile, as a kiss. "You do seem to be full of surprises, Claire McGuire."

That was truer than he knew, she thought—if he wasn't aware of her past. Her stomach went tense, but she couldn't put it off any longer. "There's something you should know. About me."

"You turn into a pumpkin at midnight."

"No, I—"

"You like to dance naked after a couple of drinks?"

She shook her head impatiently. "Six years ago, I was involved with Ken Lawrence. Engaged to be married, actually."

"How encouraging. I hadn't thought we'd reached that point yet."

She stared at him, baffled. "What point?"

"The point where we discuss any important past relationships, and, hopefully, our lack of sexually transmitted diseases. I'm clean."

This playful, flirtatious Jacob baffled her more than any of the others. "You're crazy, you know."

"My sense of humor may be somewhat warped, but I'm otherwise sane. You have a poor opinion of my business skills, though, if you thought I wouldn't know at least the basic facts about any of my employees. Even a temporary employee."

"So you *do* know what happened six years ago."

He nodded.

And he didn't care? "There may be people at the party who remember me from those days. There will be people I've never met who have opinions about me. Opinions formed by headlines and gossip. That's going to spill over onto you."

"My brothers and I have been the subjects of gossip, both in and out of print, all of our lives. My professional reputation will stand up to a little more of it. And personally, I don't give a damn."

She believed him. He really didn't care about her past. Claire felt suddenly light, almost giddy. It took all of her willpower to keep from doing something stupid, like laughing out loud. Or kissing him—one quick, smacking kiss, right on his lips.

But one quick kiss wouldn't be enough. Not with this man. "There is no 'personally' between us."

"Isn't there?" He didn't smile. His expression didn't change at all. All he did was look at her for a moment too long as the silence stretched between them, thick and unsettled. Then he went back to his office.

Leaving her with her mouth dry and her heart drumming out warnings—and something else. Something she preferred not to think about.

Four

Jacob told himself his heart wasn't pounding with anticipation when he stepped out of the shower. He was curious, that was all. He knew how appealing Claire was in her trim little jackets. What would she look like glittered up for evening?

He reached for his shirt and wondered if she had chosen basic black, or something flashier. She would know how to dress for a society party. She must have attended plenty when she was living with Ken Lawrence.

Thought of the other man made Jacob's gut tight and sick.

Psychotic. Schizoaffective Disorder, Bipolar Type, Jealous Type. That was the diagnosis of the prison psychiatrist—a diagnosis North shouldn't have been able to access, but the detective was admirably thorough.

The mouthful of syllables in the diagnosis hadn't meant much to Jacob until he looked it up and saw what it meant—delusions, mood swings. A potential for violence that had become fact, because Lawrence's central delusion had been that Claire was unfaithful to him.

From what Jacob could piece together, Ken Lawrence had probably been charming when in his manic phase—confident, clever, outgoing. Everything Jacob wasn't. That, he told himself as he zipped his dress slacks, would work to his advantage. Claire might have once fallen in love with a man who was Jacob's opposite, but she wouldn't want those traits in a lover—or a husband—now. Not after what Ken Lawrence had done.

According to North's summary of the testimony at Lawrence's trial, Claire had escaped their apartment one night when Lawrence's insane jealousy turned violent. He had gone looking for her…with a gun. He'd shown up at the home of the man he was convinced was her lover—a man she'd talked to briefly at a party the night before. A man she scarcely knew. He'd put three bullets in the poor son of a bitch, miraculously not killing him. Then he'd kept looking for Claire.

He'd found her at the apartment of her friend—a female homicide cop. Sergeant Jacqueline Muldrow had shot him before he could kill Claire.

Ken Lawrence had been seriously ill, delusional. Knowing that should have eased the anger roiling in Jacob's gut. It didn't.

The Lawrences hadn't listened when Claire had told them their son needed help. They hadn't wanted to believe he was damaged. Defective. It was a peculiar sort of love, Jacob thought, that allowed an only son to go to prison rather than admit he was mentally ill. The Lawrences had preferred to blame Claire for Ken's violence, and the result had been a prison term instead of the mental hospital where he belonged.

According to the prison psychiatrist, Lawrence had been free of symptoms at the time of his release four months ago.

The tight, hot feeling spread from Jacob's gut to his chest. He wondered if Claire knew about the psychiatrist's evaluation, if it made her feel safe. Somehow he doubted it.

Yet she wasn't afraid of men. It baffled him, but he hadn't seen a hint of fear in her around Cosmo, when she had every reason to be uneasy with a man with a prison record, one strong enough to break her in two. She wasn't afraid of Jacob, either. Wary, maybe, but her reaction seemed the instinctive feminine wariness of a woman who knew a man wanted her. Badly.

Sonia had talked to Jacob about her work with Helping Hands. He knew from those conversations that there were problems, fears, common to women who had been abused. Claire seemed curiously lacking those fears. According to North, though, she hadn't dated any man more than once or twice in the last six years.

So the fear was there, even if it didn't show, he thought as he started down the stairs. He would be careful with her. Gentle.

She was a passionate woman, an emotional woman, and that's what she would have looked for in a man—before. Jacob couldn't offer her those qualities. He was too controlled; he understood reason, not emotion. But a woman who had been hurt by a man's lack of reason and control might be drawn to those qualities. She might even find them necessary.

He wanted quite fiercely to be necessary to Claire.

Jacob didn't bother to deny the anticipation that made his steps hurry toward the small salon where he'd asked her to meet him.

She was waiting for him. And she'd chosen to wear black.

Claire stood with her back to him, looking up at the four-foot-tall painting that dominated the room. She'd done something to her hair, turning the sleek bob into glossy waves that reminded him of a forties' movie star. Her dress was slim and silky, and left her back entirely bare. The fluid line of her spine posed a wordless question about texture and taste he badly wanted to answer.

His mouth went dry. "Am I late?"

"I was a little early." She turned, that crooked smile lighting her face. "I can tell which one is you." She gestured at the painting. "That serious young man standing beside the chair, looking so stiff and reluctant. How old were you when it was painted?"

"Nine." Her dress was demure enough in front, high-necked and long-sleeved and sleek. But there was all that skin in back, so pale against the black silk.

"The baby must be Michael, and that young fellow with the angelic smile would be Luke. Michael looks a great deal like your mother."

"The woman in the painting is Lissa, Michael's mother. Not Luke's or mine."

"Oh. I, ah, knew your father had been married more than once."

"Seven times, to six women. When he died, he was two weeks away from joining bride number seven in holy matrimony. Randolph West didn't believe in casual affairs. He preferred to marry the women he slept with."

"Seven times. To six women?" She sounded incredulous.

People reacted to his father's matrimonial history in one of two ways—they either thought it wildly funny, or were appalled. He didn't know which he disliked more. "He married Luke's mother twice. Didn't you check me out before you came to work for me?''

''I asked questions about your business reputation, not your parents' private lives.''

''You must have heard about his will.''

''Well—yes, of course I'd heard about it. The stock market dipped when the terms were made public.''

''What do you know about it?''

She shrugged. ''Your father's entire fortune went into a trust administered by his personal lawyer and an assortment of corporate presidents and CEOs. The trust will be dissolved when you and your brothers marry—if you ever do.'' She tilted her head to one side. ''It must be annoying to have the business community pay as much attention to your social life as the gossip columns do.''

''Annoying is one word for it.'' He closed the distance between them. Her nearness hit him viscerally, a tightening in his gut and thighs. He wanted to answer the question posed by the slim arc of her spine. Could her skin possibly be as soft as it looked?

Control, he reminded himself. That was what he intended to offer her. A slow seduction, not a wild grab at passion.

''Did you know about your father's will?'' she asked. ''Had he always pressured you to marry?''

His mouth twisted. ''Oh, yes. We all knew. Randolph West believed in marriage. God knows he practiced his belief religiously, and, like a lot of fathers, he wanted to pass his beliefs on to his sons. Whether we liked it or not.''

''Yet none of you have married.'' She glanced once more at the painting. ''Why isn't he in the picture?''

''I don't remember. Probably he didn't have time for the sittings. When he wasn't getting married, he was working.''

''He must have been very unhappy.''

"That's an odd conclusion to reach about a man who ran everything and everyone to suit himself."

"But he kept failing, over and over, at something that mattered to him. Regardless of the reasons, it must have been hard on him."

He thought of Randolph West—big, bluff, cheerfully hedonistic, with the attention span of a two-year-old when it came to anything except business. The idea that his father might have been quietly nursing deep unhappiness over his failed marriages was absurd. And unsettling.

He spoke crisply. "If you're ready, we should leave."

"Of course." But she didn't move. "You do realize what people will assume when you bring me to this party?"

He shrugged. "Some of them, anyway. The ones who prefer supposition to facts will think you're assisting me with more personal matters than corporate backgrounds."

"That doesn't bother you?"

"No. Apparently it bothers you."

"I don't like having people think I earned my position with you on my back."

"You should be used to that. Between the jealousy of women and the covetousness of men, I doubt that you've ever had a success that some people didn't ascribe to sex instead of intelligence and hard work."

She slid him a cool look. "Am I supposed to thank you?"

"It wasn't a compliment." To please himself, he took her arm. Her skin was as soft as it looked. And warm, deliciously so. He wanted to touch more of it. He ran his hand down her arm to her wrist, circling it loosely and rubbing his thumb over the pulse point.

She pulled away. "You'll keep your hands to yourself. I don't want to feed everyone's fantasies at the party."

"Of course." But he'd felt the telltale flutter of her pulse, and was satisfied. Whether she liked it or not, she reacted to him. "Do you have a wrap?"

She did, a huge, soft cashmere shawl the same smoky-black as her stockings. She fastened it asymmetrically at one shoulder with a small gold pin. No jewels, he thought. No diamonds at her throat or ears, and no furs. She didn't want to be bought.

Maybe she would let him buy her pretty, shiny stones once she trusted him. The idea appealed to him strongly. "I'll bring the car around to the front," he said. "Wait for me there."

Jacob's car came as a surprise to Claire. Not the make—the luxury and superb engineering of a Mercedes suited him. But the car whose plush leather upholstery she slid into was a convertible, not a sensible sedan. And it was older than she was. "I'd pictured you with a new car."

"I've got one. I prefer this one. It has more personality." He shifted smoothly and started them moving. The engine had the quiet hum of power, and cool air poured from the vents. "Besides, you can't work on the new cars yourself. Everything's computerized."

Her eyebrows lifted. "You do your own mechanic work?"

"You didn't think I would enjoy getting my hands dirty, did you?"

No, she hadn't. But maybe she should have known he would prefer an old car to a new one. Look at the house he lived in—turrets and stone. "What model is this?"

"A 1957," he said, his voice heavy with that particularly masculine satisfaction that comes from owning the right toys. "I found it three years ago. Picked it up for a song. The owner didn't know what he had. The paint was ruined, the top was torn and the engine needed a complete overhaul, but the interior—'' he patted the dash affectionately ''—was in great shape.''

There was something rather sweet about his pleasure in his car. For once, he wasn't subtle or hard to read. ''Nothing like the glow we get from gloating over a real bargain, is there?''

''I don't gloat. This is a 1957 Mercedes-Benz 300Sc Cabriolet A. Do you have any idea how rare they are?''

''That, Jacob, is gloating. The same way I did the time I spotted a Dior original in a dress hanging on the sale rack at a consignment store. It had three buttons missing, the hem was coming down and there was a makeup stain on the neckline. I saw the potential, just like you did with your car. It cost twenty dollars.'' Remembered glee made her smile. ''And it was a perfect fit.''

He chuckled. ''I don't think replacing a couple of buttons is quite on a par with rebuilding an engine, but I concede your point. If I sounded half as smug as you did just now, I was definitely gloating.''

A surprisingly comfortable silence fell. Claire didn't look at him. She didn't have to. She was intensely aware of him, all those crisp, masculine angles dressed in linen and silk the color of dusk or ashes.

Jacob liked silk. She'd noticed that. On another man, the material might have looked soft. On him, it hinted at a sensuality all the more intriguing for the contrast it made with his hard body and harder features.

His shirt was unbuttoned at the collar. That hint of a loosening of his formality, of barriers slightly relaxed, was ridiculously enticing. No, she wouldn't let herself look at him. But she did glance at his hand from time to time where it rested on the gearshift. It was a strong hand, long-fingered, the palm narrow and elegant. A hard, clever hand.

She refused to let herself think about how that hand would feel on her skin.

They were headed out of Dallas proper, toward one of the many planned communities that had sprouted up like weeds crowding a water source as the complex of city and suburbs spread ever outward. The traffic was heavy once they hit the Interstate, but Jacob was a good driver, cool and competent.

No surprise there, Claire thought. He would be competent at most anything he undertook. She leaned back in the plush seat and enjoyed the ride and the long, slow slide of a summer evening on its way to night. Darkness eased in gradually at this time of year, damping the extravagant heat of the day one shade of gray at a time.

And, in spite of her good sense, she enjoyed the slow slide of heat he invoked. Skin, muscles, breath—she felt each distinctly, with a physical clarity she couldn't ignore or pretend to dislike. It didn't mean anything, she told herself, except that she was female and healthy, and her body appreciated the nearness of a healthy male body.

"This is my favorite time of day," she said.

"Why is that?"

"Oh, the shadows are all long and lazy, inviting me to slow down, take a breath. In the summer it's cool enough by now to sit outside with a drink, or putter in the garden if I'm feeling ambitious. In the winter, this time of day just begs for a fire in the fireplace. The workday is over, but it isn't time for sleep yet."

"The between time," he murmured. "Between work and sleep, daylight and dark. A time of transition. That's unusual. And interesting."

"What do you mean?"

"Most people aren't comfortable with a world that isn't all one thing or the other. They don't like ambiguity." He glanced at her. "You're more comfortable with risks than a lot of people."

She laughed uncertainly. "You're reading way too much into a simple comment. I did thrive on risks once, but I've developed some sense since then."

"Maybe. I need to brief you on what to listen for at the party," he said, changing subjects as quickly and smoothly as he changed lanes, and slowing for the exit. "I told you that Murchison is making noises about pulling out of the Stellar deal."

"He'll pay a huge forfeit if he does."

"A lot less than the two million he's committed to putting up if he stays in. He's nervous," Jacob said. "I need to know why. He's made some vague claims about rumors that contradict my data on the company. That may be true. Or someone may have his financial knickers in a twist, and he's planning on saving himself at my expense." His lips tightened. "I don't intend to allow that."

She looked at the tautness in his cheeks. No, this man wouldn't let Murchison or anyone else make him pay for their mistakes. "I haven't finished digging through the report you gave me, but he's pulled at least a million out of his regular investments in the past three months. Maybe more."

"Where's he putting it?"

"I don't know. Yet." She had some ideas, though. "Murchison is married."

He rewarded her with that sinful smile that was so startling, coming from a man who was supposed to be all ice and ambition. "Very good. Yes, the most likely reason for a married man to suddenly start hiding large sums of money is that he's anticipating a messy divorce. Which is why we're going to the party tonight."

"He's not likely to mention it."

"There will be rumors, though. There always are. Sly talk about the wife and the tennis pro, or the husband and his secretary. That's why I wanted you with me. People will look at you, see the beautiful package and not bother to look further. They'll underestimate you. If you haven't already learned how to turn that to your advantage, it's time you did. Then there's your dress."

She bristled. "What's wrong with my dress?"

"Not a thing. It's simple, elegant and you're a walking heart attack in it. Half the men there won't have enough blood left in their brains to mind their tongues the way they ought to. Another benefit of taking you to the party."

Temper crackled, a quick flame she tried to squelch. And failed. "You did warn me that you used whatever talents your employees possess. Is there anyone in particular you'd like me to seduce for you?"

"Other than myself, you mean? No," he said thoughtfully. "I prefer you to concentrate on me."

She wished that didn't make her want to laugh. Time to change the subject, she decided. "Tell me what I should know about the Murchisons that wasn't in the file."

He slid her one of those long, unreadable looks of his, but complied. For the next twenty minutes she did a fair job of pretending she had her mind firmly on business…instead of wondering if she was sure that business was all she wanted from this man.

Five

The sun squatted on the horizon, round and fat and red, when they reached their destination, flooding the air with color. Murchison lived in a development zoned for the wealthy. Each house sat in isolated splendor in a landscape of rolling green studded with the knobby growth of oaks and the massed darkness of clustered pines, near-black now in the fading light.

Claire wished they could stop long enough to put the top down, then take off again, go flying through that thick, orange air. Nerves jittered under her skin as she climbed out of the car.

Who would she see tonight that she hadn't seen in six years?

It wasn't really the people she might meet that made her heart jerk in her chest and her skin feel too tight. It was a ghost. The ghost of the girl she'd been at twenty-two—that heedless, headstrong girl who had dipped into passion with all the reckless arrogance of youth.

She had been so sure. Of herself, of her heart. At first.

Memories shivered over her. She shoved them down.

Most of the guests had already arrived, judging by the number of cars choking the road that led up the small hill to the house. Jacob parked at the base of the hill. The night was unseasonably mild, pleasant enough that Claire unfastened her shawl and let it slip to her elbows as they started toward the lights and music coming from the big house.

"Mariachi music?" she said, straining to sound calm and untroubled. "An odd choice for a Christmas party."

"Laura Murchison is Mexican-American." Though cars crowded both sides of the narrow road, there was plenty of room in the middle of it for pedestrians. Yet Jacob walked close, close enough that the sleeve of his shirt brushed her arm with every step.

"The wife he may be planning on ditching?"

"Or who might be planning on ditching him." He glanced down at her. "Nervous?"

She would have eaten worms before admitting it. "Of course not."

"Perhaps you could try picturing everyone in their underwear."

"Wh-what?" she sputtered, caught between a laugh and indignation.

"That's the advice my father gave me once when I had to give a speech. I was so terrified I thought I might throw up before I got a sentence out."

"You?" She gave him an incredulous look.

"I was the valedictorian for my sixth-grade class."

"Your elementary school had valedictorians?"

"Silly, isn't it?" His eyes looked oddly luminous in the soft light. He might have been smiling. "It was a private school. I didn't persuade my father to let me attend public school until the next year. After that experience, I never again made the mistake of competing for the top honors." He shook his head. "Thanks to my father's advice, I did make it through the speech without disgracing myself."

"You didn't puke."

"Exactly. No one laughed when they were supposed to, though."

She smiled, thinking of a sober, serious twelve-year-old Jacob, already possessed of that sneaky sense of humor. "I don't suppose you tried smiling to give them a hint when you told a joke."

"Are you kidding? My face was frozen with fear."

"According to your brother, you were born with a poker face."

"I warned you about believing him. He wasn't there when I was born, so what does he know?" He reached out to ring the doorbell

They had reached the front without her noticing. And Claire *was* relaxed now, the sick knot of tension dissipated, when their host came forward to greet them. Jacob had done that, with his story of terror in the sixth grade.

Kindness. It wasn't what she'd expected from the Iceman, but she was beginning to think it lay beneath every one of his confusing personas. He let his housekeeper bully him, and renovated his home so his assistant wouldn't have to climb the stairs. He hired an ex-con and offered to put up the capital for the man to start his own business. And he helped a nervous woman relax, when he shouldn't even have known she was nervous.

Kindness, she was learning, could be devastatingly attractive.

Andy Murchison was a tall man with thinning hair, a small paunch, and a lovely, much-younger wife. He greeted

Jacob a little too heartily, paid more attention to Claire's breasts than her face and didn't offer to shake hands. "So this is Sonia's replacement," he said, smiling broadly. "I always did say you had good taste, West. Damned good taste."

"I pride myself on finding top-notch employees," Jacob said. "How pleasant to have it acknowledged. You must have heard of Ms. McGuire's skills. Or perhaps you already knew her?"

"Haven't had that pleasure until tonight. Though the name is familiar..." His glance sharpened, turning speculative.

And so, she thought, *it begins.*

He was aware of her. Whether he was talking to a woman who had briefly been his lover, or discussing football and stock prices with potential investors, Jacob felt the pull of Claire's presence. He'd catch the bright hint of her laughter above the other voices, glimpse the smooth slope of her shoulder or the hot flame of her hair through a parting in the crowd.

Even when he couldn't see or hear her, he knew where she was. Like the slow, subtle pull of the moon on the ocean, she drew him. He didn't approve. A man could drown in a tide this strong and heedless.

But his disapproval didn't seem to matter. He was aware of her.

Staying beside her would have made them look more like a couple. Because she disliked that, didn't want people to think he had purchased her body along with her business skills, he'd left her on her own after the first few introductions.

It wouldn't make much difference, he knew. Most people preferred their assumptions to facts, and those who didn't think he and his assistant were already lovers would believe it was only a matter of time.

They'd be right.

Jacob hadn't lied when he told her he wanted her here to act as a second set of eyes and ears. He did. But he'd had another reason, too. He'd wanted to see how she handled herself amid the social piranhas. If he married her, the current buzz of gossip would rise to brass-band levels.

If she was still nervous, it didn't show. She chatted and listened and mingled with every appearance of ease, ignoring the speculative glances. She shone. It wasn't just the stunning face, or the sheer, sexual grace of her body. There was something about her, something special he couldn't put into words.

How many of these people knew her? Quite a few had heard of her, he thought, judging by the stiff way some reacted. He saw the way men's eyes followed her, the way women smiled at her too brightly. Or not at all. And he didn't like it. He wanted to be beside her, deflecting the sly glances, shielding her from what he'd brought her here to face.

Damn. He swirled his drink gently, knowing she stood fifteen feet away, talking to an older couple. Not looking at her, but knowing.

"Some people have all the luck," an envious voice said.

"Wade." Jacob acknowledged the other man with a nod. Bill Wade was a good friend of Murchison's. "How's Emily?"

"Fine." But the man's eyes were on Claire. She laughed at something the gray-haired man beside her said, her head thrown back slightly to reveal the clean line of her throat.

No diamonds, Jacob thought. But they would look beautiful gracing that throat.

"Why haven't you introduced me to your new assistant yet?"

"Because you're a happily married man?" Jacob said dryly.

"No one is *that* happily married." Wade was a chubby, forty-something-year-old man with an unfortunate fondness for custom-made boots, flashy Western shirts and bolo ties. He looked like an accountant dressed up to play cowboy. "Not that she would look at me twice with you in the picture. But a man can dream."

"I'd hate to attend your funeral, Wade. Unlike our hostess tonight, Emily does have a possessive streak. And a temper."

He chuckled. "That she does. 'Course, I like a little jealousy in a woman. Shows there's some fire."

"Mmm." Claire started to leave the group she'd been talking to. A man with a thick mustache and the controlling interest in a regional supermarket chain tried to detain her. She detached him expertly, smiling while she did it.

"Now, Andy says he prefers the shy ones, like Laura. Still waters, and all that. I don't know, though." He chuckled. "The way he's been eyeing that, ah, assistant of yours, he might be willing to make an exception. Don't think Claire McGuire is exactly the quiet type."

Jacob sipped his watery drink, looking over the heads of the crowd until he spotted Claire. "Murchison has a wandering eye, does he?"

"You don't have to worry," Wade said hastily. "He wouldn't—and even if he would, why would *she?* Andy ain't exactly up to your weight, if you know what I mean."

"Hmm." Jacob wondered if unearthing a scrap or two of gossip was worth wading through the midden of Wade's conversation. He looked away to pick out his next target. And stiffened.

"Did I say something wrong? Hey, West, what are you…"

Wade was still talking, but Jacob wasn't listening. He was moving. Fast.

The Lawrences were here. And they'd found Claire.

Dammit, he should have anticipated this. But he hadn't known the Lawrences were part of the Murchisons' set. He'd been to a couple of other parties here, and the Lawrences hadn't been present—but those had been smaller parties, not a big bash like this.

Claire didn't see them at first. But she must have felt something, or noticed the distress on her hostess's face. She turned. Jacob heard her reaction clearly from twelve feet away.

"Well, hell."

Jim and Sue Lawrence looked eerily the same, more like siblings than husband and wife. Each was slim, tanned, with patrician features and silvery-blond hair. Each thin, unlined face wore the same expression—anger, gathering rapidly into fury.

Jacob reached Claire's side just as the storm broke.

"You bitch." Sue Lawrence's face wasn't smooth anymore. Or pretty. "How dare you show your face here, with decent people?"

"Sue," Claire said wearily, "are you sure you want to make a scene?"

"Is it not worth the trouble unless you have the TV cameras to preen for? To tell your lies to."

Jacob spoke quietly. "Jim, maybe you should take Sue over to the bar and get her another drink."

Jim Lawrence's gaze didn't move from Claire. "Stay out of this. It isn't any of your business."

"Claire is with me."

That got his attention. "With you? What the hell were

you thinking of, bringing this tramp here? Don't you know who she is?''

"I know she's my employee." Jacob still spoke quietly, but he let a trace of warning coat his voice. Claire was with him, and he wasn't going to let anyone insult her. "If you can't control yourself and your wife, you'd better leave."

"Please," Laura Murchison said. "Please, let's all stay calm."

Sue Lawrence shot her a quick glance, some of the venom she felt for Claire spilling over onto the younger woman. "You shouldn't have invited her here. How dare you invite her here!"

"She didn't know." That was Claire. "I came with Jacob, like he said. Sue, please. It's time to stop working so hard at blaming me. Ken needs your help, your support. He doesn't need—"

"Don't you tell me what my son needs!" Her voice rose shrilly. "He was all right, he was fine, until you got your claws into him—lying to him, cheating, flaunting yourself and your lovers—"

"No. He wasn't all right. He hid it well, but he wasn't all right."

"He—he—" Sue Lawrence's lips quivered. Her eyes filled. And her hand flashed out.

Jacob caught her wrist just before she connected, claws out, with Claire's cheek. "Jim," he said, not taking his eyes off the woman whose frail wrist he held. Hatred shone in Sue Lawrence's eyes as clearly as the tears that were starting to trickle down one thin cheek.

"It's your fault," she said, her voice hoarse. She seemed unaware that Jacob still held her wrist. "It's all your fault."

Andy Murchison came up then. "Hey, everyone, the bartender's getting lonely, so why don't we all move along, give him something to do?"

At last Jim Lawrence moved, his body as stiff as his face, taking his wife's outstretched hand and pulling her away. He didn't speak—to her, to Jacob, to the guests who watched with all the ghoulish fascination of bystanders at a freeway accident. He put his arm around Sue's shoulders and walked away with her, all without saying a word.

"Laura," Murchison said, his face tight with displeasure. "Why didn't you do something?"

"I can't imagine what you thought she could do." Claire's lifted chin aimed a challenge at Murchison.

He looked at her as if he'd found a roach crawling through the pretty desserts set out on the buffet table near the house.

"You want to be careful of what you say," Jacob told him, and did what he'd been wanting to do all along. He put his arm around Claire.

She was shaking. The discovery infuriated him. The tremors were fine, so slight he hadn't seen them, hadn't guessed what the encounter had cost her.

"Jacob," Murchison said, "you must have known your date's presence could cause problems. I think you owe me an explanation."

"And I think you owe me two million dollars." He turned his back on the man, forcing Claire to move with him, heading toward the sliding doors at the back of the huge living room. They'd been left open in deference to the mild weather.

"You can let go now," she said as soon as they were away from Murchison. "I'm all right."

"I'm not."

Six

Claire did try to pull away, but Jacob's arm tightened on her shoulders. He didn't give her much choice, short of creating a second scene, and she wasn't up to that. So she let him steer her out the glass doors onto the veranda…but that didn't explain why she kept moving with him away from the veranda, kept moving away from the house and toward the woods that bordered the yard.

There was a path. It was fully dark now, but tiny white lights were strung along the border of a trail coyly graveled to look almost natural. The path wandered off into the woods, and they went with it.

Jacob's arm around her shoulders was firm, but not suggestive. He was offering comfort and support, not seduction. And heat was pooling in her belly, a thick languor that built, pulse by pulse, step by step as the trees closed around them. He was solid and strong. Mixed with the green odor of pine and damp earth, she thought she could smell him—a faint, rich, masculine scent.

She should pull away. She wasn't so shaken by the encounter with Sue Lawrence that she needed his arm for support. Sue's rancor had been unpleasant, but nothing new.

In a moment she would move away. In just another moment.

The sounds of the party faded behind them, muffled by trunks, leaves and the stony ground of the path that wound downward, away from the house at the top of the hill. Overhead was darkness, the stars and moon shrouded by the tree limbs arching above them. At Claire's feet those tiny lights beckoned. Fairy lights.

Weren't fairy lights supposed to be dangerous? Glowing, witchy promises that tempted mortals beyond safe boundaries, luring the foolish into realms where sense and order couldn't follow.

She shivered.

"Cold?"

"No." She regretted her quick, too-honest answer, and at last managed to pull away. This time he didn't try to stop her. "It's just reaction."

His voice was tight, as if he were still exerting control over emotions she couldn't guess. "I didn't know the Lawrences would be here."

"How could you have? I doubt Murchison presented you with a guest list."

"I should have considered the possibility. I don't make a habit of being unprepared. Were there other lovers?"

"What?" Her feet stopped as she gaped at him.

"When you were with Lawrence, did you have other lovers? Or was it all a product of his delusions?"

The hurt was sharper than it should have been. Her eyes

alarmed her by stinging, and she started walking again, as quickly as she could in heels on the unlevel path. "I thought you were being kind, taking me away from that scene. I didn't realize you just wanted to interrogate me privately."

"I'm not a kind man."

Wasn't he? He'd stood beside her while Sue Lawrence spilled her usual assortment of threats and blame and garbage. Why, if he thought Sue was telling the truth?

He kept pace with her easily enough and, for the moment, in silence. From somewhere up ahead came the quiet gurgle of water chuckling to itself.

"Why did you let Sue Lawrence speak to you that way?" he asked.

"At what point did you think I had a choice?"

"You were gentle with her."

The prick of memory or guilt made her speak sharply. "Her son's crazy. She's entitled to feel bad about that. I may not like the way she goes about venting her feelings, but she can't really hurt me."

"Then why were you shaking?"

Damn him for noticing. "Repressed temper."

"No. You were upset."

"I'm getting upset all over again. None of this is any of your business, except to the extent that it affects you because you brought me here. Not," she added pointedly, "that I wanted you to."

"I wondered how long it would take for you to mention that."

"Would you have insisted I come with you if you'd known the Lawrences would be here?"

"Possibly. At least I could have made an informed decision. I don't intend to be caught unprepared again, which is why I'm asking you questions you don't want to answer. Just how crazy is Ken Lawrence?''

She intended to just keep walking, but a piece of gravel turned beneath her foot, throwing her off balance. He was there, steadying her with a hand on her elbow.

He could have turned it into an excuse for an embrace. He didn't. And she was furious to discover a twinge of disappointment. ''I tell you what. I'll answer your questions if you'll answer mine, one for one. I'll go first.''

There was enough fairy light for her to see his slight smile. ''All right. What do you want to know?''

''What does it matter to you whether I was faithful to Ken, or cheated on him four times a night?''

He was silent a moment too long. ''I want to know if you'll be faithful to me after I take you to bed.''

''Arrogant, aren't you?'' Her heart pounded too hard. With fear? She turned and started to move away.

He stopped her, clasping her shoulder firmly.

''I told you to keep your hands to yourself. I meant it.''

His voice was cool and unmoved. His hand, too, remained unmoved—but not cool. ''We're at the end of the path. Unless you want to go wading, you need to stop here.''

She blinked. Right in front of her, no more than a couple of steps away, was the water she'd heard, a merry trickle of a stream borne of the heavy rains they'd had lately.

''I answered your question,'' he said. ''Now it's my turn. Were you faithful to Lawrence?''

''I could say yes, but why would you believe me?''

''Why would you lie? The woman depicted by the media wouldn't bother to, not over this. She would be proud of her ability to captivate any number of men.''

''I'm not the woman I was six years ago.''

''That doesn't answer my question.''

For a moment, pain rose from the past to swamp the present, hard and blinding, just as it had been during those dark days when she'd lost the casual certainty that was innocence, one betrayal at a time. "We were going to be married." Her voice echoed the bewilderment she'd felt so long ago. "Of course I was faithful."

"Lawrence's jealousy was wholly irrational, then."

He made it a statement, not a question. Maybe that was why she didn't notice him moving closer until he stopped, his hand still on her shoulder, his body inches from hers.

Jacob's expression was always hard to read. With his face underlit by the faint glow from the fairy lights, he looked utterly mysterious. Unknowable, almost sinister. "I—I liked to flirt," she said. "I liked men, but I never— I would never…he knew that. I could have sworn he knew that when he asked me to marry him." Pain and the past both had to be swallowed so she could steady her voice. "That was your second question. You owe me one."

He reached up and cupped her other shoulder. "Ask."

She opened her mouth—and closed it again. Questions flew through her mind, quick and small, massive and important. All dangerous. Questions opened doors, and suddenly she didn't want any more doors open between herself and this man. She shook her head.

"How sick is Lawrence?"

"It's not your turn to ask a question."

"All right. I won't ask if I can kiss you, then."

She stiffened, expecting an assault—hard, driving, determined. Ready for one.

He tricked her.

His hands didn't drag her to him. His mouth didn't crush down on hers, forcing her to feel more than she wanted…giving her something to fight against. Instead his head lowered slowly, with all the offhand inevitability of that little stream chuckling its way downhill. She could have pulled away.

She didn't. Because he'd just answered one of those questions she hadn't dared ask. One she should have asked herself.

Why had she let him bring her here, away from the others?

For this. Her eyelids drifted low, almost closing as his lips drifted onto hers, and settled. She'd come with him for this.

How had he known she needed this, the slow, subtle lesson in his taste he offered as his mouth rocked gently on hers? The smooth spread of his hands on her bare back as his fingers stretched to hold more of her. And not enough.

She heard a sound—more than a gasp, not quite a moan. And knew it came from her. Why hadn't she known how devastating the gradual wooing of her mouth could be? A sensual courting that left her free, always, to break away. And made her crave more. Deeper, hotter.

Her lips quivered open, and he came inside. His hands slid down her arms, moved to her waist. The muscles of her inner thighs quivered. Fire curled in a sweet, hot ball, low in her belly. Her eyes stayed open as her hands reached for him, found him.

The wall of his chest was hard beneath the nubby silk of his shirt, as hard as the unreadable mask of his face. The skin at the base of his neck was rough and warm. The feel of his hair, cool and short and soft, mingled with the musk of his skin and the green smell of the woods around them. Her fingers found the pulse in his throat. It drummed out a message at odds with the careful precision of his hands— the only hint she found that he hungered as she did.

But it was honest, that small physical revelation. She

closed her eyes, reading him better with hands and mouth than she could with vision. Speaking to him the same way.

Let go, she said wordlessly as her hands began a restless questioning of their own. *Want me,* her mouth said as she tilted her head to deepen the kiss. *Lose yourself,* her heart said. *Take this and lose yourself in it.* But she didn't know if her heart spoke to him. Or to her.

She felt desire hit him—the quick, hard quiver of muscles across his chest. A harsh, in-drawn breath. His hands clamping suddenly just under her rib cage, bruisingly hard. Possessive. Something clicked into place inside her, something nameless and necessary. She pressed against him, and found need.

And he let her go.

Air, cool and unwelcome, replaced him all along her front. She wanted to curse or to cry, but was too confused to do either. Slowly she opened her eyes.

He'd moved back several paces. If he was struggling as she was for sense and sanity, it didn't show. Except for a slight hurry in the lift and fall of his chest, he looked unmoved. But he didn't speak. For long moments they stared at each other, moonlight and questions between them, fairyglow and earth at their feet.

"What happened just now?" she asked, then winced at her foolishness. What had happened? Just a kiss. A kiss that had sent everything sliding sideways, tilting her world.

He didn't answer her silly question. "Did I hurt you?"

Not yet, she thought, then realized he was talking about the way his hands had gripped her. "No. Is that why you changed your mind? Because you were afraid you'd hurt me?"

"I didn't think you'd want me to take you here in the dirt. Was I wrong?"

She was glad he'd said that. It made her angry, and anger

was easy and understandable. She started back the way they'd come, dimly surprised that her body obeyed and moved normally. But he stood in the center of the path, his big body blocking her, the trees crowding them too closely for her to go around him.

She stopped and looked up at him. "Are you going to stand there and stare at me all night?"

"This was a mistake." He seemed to be speaking as much to himself as to her. "It's going to complicate things."

That he was right didn't ease the sharp sting of his words. She should agree with him, should point out that they were adults and could put this moment of misplaced lust behind them and work together. And if he'd decided he didn't want her after all, that was all for the best.

Ten minutes ago, that was what she'd wanted. To keep things on a businesslike basis between them. Not now. Now she knew the feel of his mouth, the clutch in her belly when his hands had gripped her so fiercely. She wanted it again, wanted to see if the world slid crazily, then clicked into place once more when she was in his arms.

But now he was stepping aside, turning his body so she could go up the path ahead of him. Standing aside and letting her pass without touching him. Telling her without words that he intended to give her exactly what she'd wanted...ten minutes ago.

A mistake. Jacob hadn't intended to tell her that. The words had slipped out as soon as the truth of them had pressed itself into a mind still blank with shock. Those words stayed with him as they waited at the front of the house for his car to be brought up.

Thank God she didn't seem to feel the need to talk things out the way so many women did. That had been one of the few things he'd disliked about Maggie, her tendency to pick apart emotions like a coach reviewing the films of his team's misplays. Discussion wouldn't mend matters. It wouldn't undo his mistake.

He'd been aware of Claire before. Now, after tasting her, the awareness was ten times more acute. He felt her silent presence beside him, could almost count her breaths. He didn't want to look at her, but good manners obliged him to open the door for her.

She looked pale. And damn near as jumpy as he felt. "Could we put the top down?"

It was the last thing he'd expected her to say. "It will mess up your hair."

"I know how to use a hairbrush. Look, if you don't want to bother, just say so."

"I'll put it down." The wind would be noisy without the top, loud enough to make conversation difficult. That appealed to him as much as the flight and freedom of driving open to the world. He unfastened the catches and folded back the top, his hands performing the familiar task without requiring any of his attention.

She commanded that.

Claire slid into the car gracefully, but even so, her dress rode up, giving him a glimpse of smooth white thigh. He wanted to taste the skin behind her knees.

He was scowling when he sat behind the steering wheel.

Jacob had two ways of dealing with tension when it built too high to ignore. He either worked it off physically—in the gym, sparring with Cosmo, swimming laps—or he climbed in this car with the top down, and let speed and wind blow a little calm back inside him.

Tonight it didn't work. The air smelled fresh and wild away from the congestion of the city. Usually that helped.

But even jamming down the accelerator when they reached the Interstate didn't soothe him.

Neither did the silence he'd thought he wanted. She hadn't said a word, and it was driving him crazy.

Dammit, it wasn't as if he'd mauled her. She'd been vulnerable after the confrontation with the Lawrences, but he'd been careful with her...right up until the moment when he hadn't been. When need had surged so strongly it had wiped out everything else. Like a tree hit by a flood and dragged from its banks, its roots still tangled in the earth that should have held it, he'd been yanked out of his control.

Shock had stopped him then, not any remnant of self-discipline. Pure, icy shock had slapped him in the face with what he'd done. And what he'd been about to do.

A man who couldn't control himself with a woman couldn't be trusted. Not by her, not by himself.

The traffic grew heavier, forcing him to slow. They were nearly to the exit that would take them to Garland. Still she didn't speak.

He'd had about enough of her sitting there without saying a word. "If you still want to get your cat, you'd better give me directions."

"Take the loop to the Cates exit, then head north to Valley Mills." Her voice was cool and clipped, barely audible over the rush of air. "Go three blocks and turn left on Delmar. My house is 1110."

"It's not as if I attacked you," he growled suddenly. She'd wanted him. Whatever other mistakes he'd made that night, he wasn't wrong about that. Her body had turned fluid and soft against his. Her hands had sought him out. "You were willing. More than willing. So if you're waiting for an apology, you—what did you say?" The wind had caught her voice and whipped it away.

She didn't answer. He spared her one quick glance and caught her profile, facing forward, her hair whipping madly around her face.

He scowled. "You're laughing."

"Sorry. I thought—oh, never mind what I thought. I understand now. You're upset because you got a little carried away, aren't you?"

A *little* carried away? His fingers tightened bruise-hard on the steering wheel. He'd lost control. He'd thought that would be the worst thing he could do with Claire, but she sure as hell didn't seem upset about it.

If she didn't want his money, didn't want reason and control from him, what did he have that she could possibly need?

Her mirth had faded. "Is this going to make problems for us? In working together, I mean."

"No." He wouldn't look at her. "No problem. I kissed you, you kissed me back. We're adults. We don't have to let it interfere with our business relationship."

"Then why are you so angry?"

Good question.

The wind rushing by now smelled of concrete and exhaust, not pine and dirt. The darkness was spoiled by the countless lights of the city, strobed by headlights and neon. There was no peace here. There was no peace in his thoughts, either, and somehow the bright, crowded silence of the city made it impossible to avoid those thoughts.

He'd been a breath away from pushing her down on the ground, pushing up her skirt and taking her there, fast and hard and hot. And she wondered why he was angry?

Claire needed a man she could trust. He didn't trust himself. It was time to step back, reappraise the situation and his goal.

He didn't want to.

Jacob was not a simple man. Complexity and contradiction had been bred into him by the chaos of his childhood, but he'd learned to impose order on uncertainty by setting goals. Once he'd chosen a target, he became remarkably simple and direct. Everything he was, everything he had, went toward accomplishing his goal.

He wanted Claire McGuire more than he had ever wanted a woman. He also wanted to push her away—out of his house, out of his life. Out of his head.

It was that kiss, he thought. That damned kiss. He didn't want to step back. He didn't want to go forward, either.

Dammit to hell.

Her voice broke into his thoughts. "My house is just ahead, on the left. The one with the circular driveway."

He saw it. Her cousin hadn't left the porch light on for her, but there were lights on inside the house. Jacob pulled into the driveway and shut off the ignition. "I'll come in with you."

She clicked open her seat belt and slid him an amused glance. "I was going to ask."

"There are lights on inside," he observed as he rounded the front of the car.

"Danny is house-sitting for me." There was a hint of challenge in the look she gave him, a certain stiffness in her posture as she started for the door. It occurred to him that she expected him to be jealous.

Claire had reason to fear a man's jealousy. "Best not to leave a house empty," he said mildly, keeping pace with her.

"That's what I thought." She slid him another glance, as if checking out his reaction. "Danny is my cousin." She had her key out and was reaching for the door.

"The one you grew up with?"

"Yes, he…that's odd."

The door had swung inward the moment she touched the knob, spilling dim yellow light onto the porch.

Jacob acted instinctively, shoving in front of her.

"Jacob." He heard the fear in her voice. "If—if someone's in there, we should call the police."

"Good idea. My cell phone is in the car." With one hand, he shoved the door open the rest of the way. With the other he kept her from moving forward. "Claire. Stay here."

"Danny's in there."

"Maybe. I'll find out. Go call the police." He listened intently, but heard nothing.

A window directly opposite the front door looked out on a small atrium lit by small floodlights. There was a hall at one end of the entry, a doorway at the other. More light came from that doorway. "Stay here," he repeated.

She didn't argue. She didn't obey him, either, but at least she stayed behind him.

Jacob reached the doorway and stopped dead.

It had been a pleasant living area. The walls were a cool white that showed off the dark wood of shelves; there was glass and brass and paler, unstained wood. Deep-cushioned sofas the blue of the ocean faced each other across a celery-colored carpet.

Now it was chaos. A tall entertainment unit had been toppled, spilling its contents helter-skelter across that pale carpet. A lamp had been hurled into the brick fireplace, a glass-topped table smashed, leaving shards of glass sparkling in the light from the remaining lamp.

There was blood.

Blood, splattered obscenely on one white wall. Trailing in a sad, wavering line across that pale carpet. Leading to the body sprawled across the arched doorway at the other end of the room.

Claire made a choked noise caught between a scream and a sob. A name that strangled in her throat.

They'd found Danny.

Seven

The surgical waiting room was beige. Carpet, couch and chairs were the color of wet sand; the end tables were blond wood, the walls off-white. A few spots of color sprouted, germ-like, to disturb the room's antiseptic beigeness. The lamp on the table was orange. The covers on the flock of limp magazines scattered around held more secret colonies of color.

The scrubs on the surgeon who'd just entered were blue.

He was speaking to an older couple who had been waiting here when she and Jacob arrived. The man was stout, with a shiny bald spot on the top of his head and a stoic expression. He held his wife's hand tightly. She was plump and pale, with beauty-shop hair, a crisp green dress and the dried tracks of tears on her cheeks.

Only serious injury sent people into surgery after midnight.

Danny had been in surgery for...Claire's eyes drifted to the clock on the wall directly above the surgeon's head.

Only forty-five minutes? No, the clock must be broken. Surely hours had passed since she had come here to wait...with Jacob.

He hadn't left her side since they found Danny, bloody and beaten, in her home. He sat beside her now, answering the questions put to him by the police detective. Claire wasn't listening. She had already answered those same questions, and more.

Jacob had quietly taken charge when necessary, helping her thread the paperwork maze once they reached the hospital. Quiet the rest of the time, but always right beside her, his presence as soothing as the strong silence of a mountain. He'd even taken care of her cat—or tried to.

She glanced at his hand. Three raw stripes decorated the back of it. Sheba had rebuked Jacob for trying to catch her, then escaped when the paramedics arrived.

It was stupid to be worrying about her cat. Sheba could take care of herself for one night. But when Claire pushed those thoughts aside, she started thinking about Danny again, lying on the operating table with a piece of his skull removed...

The woman in the green dress gave a little cry. Claire's gaze darted to her. She didn't mean to intrude, but, selfishly and superstitiously, she wanted the woman to learn that their wait had ended happily, as if that would be a preview of the moment when Danny's surgeon came to talk to Claire.

The woman clasped her hands together over her mouth. She was crying. But the man was grinning, slapping the surgeon on the back.

Their news had been good.

"Claire? Did you hear the question?"

"What?" Claire blinked, focusing on the woman who'd spoken. Jacqueline Muldrow was tall and thin, with black hair cut close to her skull, a strong face and a Hershey's bar complexion—smooth, rich chocolate. She was utterly lacking in vanity. Claire doubted that Jackie's curly lashes had ever come within blinking distance of a mascara wand. She'd been Claire's best friend since the eighth grade, but Jackie wasn't here as a friend tonight. She was here as Sergeant Muldrow, the detective who had helped put Ken Lawrence behind bars six years ago.

Claire prayed she could do that again. Quickly. "Sorry, Jackie, I wasn't listening."

"Other than the letter you gave me, has Ken Lawrence made any attempt to contact you since he was released?"

"No. Danny said—" She had to stop and swallow. "He said there was a rose, a red rose, on the porch this morning. I told you that."

Jackie's eyes softened. "Sugar, men have been strewing flowers in your path ever since you got tits. A rose on your porch doesn't prove anything."

"But it was a red rose. No note, just the single rose. It was him. You *know* that, Jackie. You know he always used to bring me one red rose." One perfect rose, because their love was perfect. Because they were meant to be one. She shivered.

Jacob took her hand, the gesture at odds with his crisp, detached voice. "The court won't care what the sergeant knows, Claire. She needs proof."

"I know. I know that, and a rose isn't proof. And the letter he sent was printed and unsigned. But it was him." Her hand tightened on his. Ken had attacked Danny, had nearly killed him. And it was her fault. "When Danny wakes up, he'll be able to identify Ken."

Jackie made a noncommittal sound. Jacob didn't say anything.

Claire bit her lip. The older couple was leaving, the man's arm around his wife. The surgeon had already vanished through the door marked Hospital Personnel Only.

They'd had good news. She would, too. "Danny *will* wake up."

"He's got a good surgeon."

Claire grabbed hold of hope as quickly as it was tossed out. "Yes, you said he was supposed to be one of the best."

When they'd reached the hospital soon after the ambulance, the emergency room doctor had briefed her quickly. With a depressed skull fracture and a punctured lung, Danny's need for surgery had been immediate and acute. There had been no time to choose a surgeon, but Jacob had checked out the neurosurgeon on call.

"Even once Danny wakes up," Jackie said tactfully, "he may not remember the attack. Head injuries are funny."

Claire tried not to think about all the ways head injuries could be "funny." Danny might not remember other things, like how to drive a car or tie his shoes. She released Jacob's hand and pushed to her feet. "We'll have to wait and see, won't we?"

"In the meantime, I can talk to Ken Lawrence." Jackie stood and slipped her notebook into a pocket in her wrinkled blazer. "See if he has an alibi."

Jacob rose. He was only a couple of inches taller than Jackie. "Has the weapon been found?"

"I'll check with the guys on-scene, and let you know. But don't get your hopes up. Even the most reckless perps know about fingerprints."

"Ken's not reckless," Claire said flatly. "He's crazy."

"Hold on." Jackie held up one long, blunt-nailed hand. "Lawrence is the obvious suspect, but we can't close the

book on other possibilities, not yet. Danny could have en-
emies of his own, or he might have surprised a thief.''

"Come on, Jackie, you know it was Ken! That wasn't a
regular break-in. Nothing was taken, and the living room
was trashed.'' As if Danny had tried to fight Ken.

She'd told him—oh, she'd told him not to.

"Hey.'' Jackie caught her shoulders in a quick, one-
armed hug. "Do I tell you how to make money for your
clients? You do your job, and I'll do mine. If it was
Lawrence, I'll get him. Don't worry about that. But I have
to keep an open mind, or I might miss something. Has
Danny made anyone mad lately?''

She shrugged. "You know Danny. Everyone likes him.''

"Mmm. I sent a patrol officer to speak to his father.''

"Fine. If he can get Uncle Lou to answer the door,
maybe he'll come see how his son is.'' Claire's mouth
twisted. "He didn't answer the phone when I called. It's
Friday night. He's probably passed out.''

"I guess Danny and his father haven't been getting
along.''

"No worse than usual.''

"But he doesn't usually move in with you. His father
kick him out?''

"You think—no. No, you're way off base. Uncle Lou
can be a mean drunk, but he's mean with words, not his
fists.''

"I take it Danny isn't working.''

"No. He's started going to AA, Jackie, but it's going to
take time. No one wants to take a chance on someone with
his employment history. When he's been sober longer—''

"That's just like you,'' a belligerent male voice said.
"Tryin' to blame the boy's screwups on booze. Can't admit
it's your fault, can you? All your fault.''

She jerked and turned to the door. And sighed. "Uncle Lou."

Jacob had guessed the newcomer's identity before Claire spoke. The man's features were a blurred and ruined male version of hers, and his hair had probably once been the same flaming red. His bloodshot eyes gave him the look of an angry boar, an impression heightened by the graying bristles on his cheeks and chin.

He brought the stink of stale beer in with him. "Don't want me here, do you? Didn't even have the courtesy to call me, let me know my boy's in surgery with his head bashed in." His mood shifted with alcohol-slippery suddenness into tears. "Danny. My poor Danny."

"I called," Claire said quietly. "You didn't hear the phone ring."

"You've always been bad for him. Taking him away from me, settin' him against me..." He shifted back to anger. "Meddling bitch. You put him here. You and your—"

"Be careful," Jacob said, his voice icy. "Better yet, be quiet."

He squinted sullenly at Jacob. "Who're you?"

Claire's cop friend moved between them. "Mr. McGuire, I'm Sergeant Muldrow. Would you mind answering some questions?" With a deft application of official courtesy, she steered him out into the hall.

Jacob would rather have hit the man, but the sergeant's technique was probably better. Claire was pale, her skin tight under haunted eyes. She didn't need a scene. What she did need was someone who understood all this emotional business. Someone who could help.

Unfortunately all she had at the moment was him. "Are you all right?"

"Family." Her grimace may have been meant as a smile.

"They can be the very devil, can't they? Uncle Lou is a trial at the best of times."

"What happened was not your fault."

"Wasn't it?" She lifted stark eyes to his. "I knew Ken might come looking for me. He's supposed to be okay now. He got treatment while he was in prison, but I can't make myself believe in his 'recovery.' His letter scared me, and I ran off. But I left Danny there..." Her lips quivered. "Dammit, I told him to call the cops if Ken came around. I told him."

She was blaming herself, and he had no idea how to get through to her. "You aren't responsible for what Lawrence did."

"Maybe not, but I know Danny. He has this idea that he owes me. I've helped him sometimes, sure. But the fact is, I owe him, not the other way around. Uncle Lou is right. I *was* bad for Danny, back when we were kids. I..." She shook her head. "Never mind. You don't want to hear a lot of ancient history."

"It won't hurt me to listen." He might not know how to go about offering any real comfort, but he could listen. "Why do you think you were bad for Danny?"

"Because I was." She passed a shaky hand over her hair, which had lost its neat waves when they rode with the top down. It rioted quietly around her face now, making his palms itch with the urge to touch it.

He put his hands into his pockets. "When you were a young hell-raiser, you mean?"

"I told you that, didn't I?" She managed a smile, but it slid away quickly. "When I was a teenager I put my mother through hell. And I dragged Danny right along with me."

"He's responsible for his own choices."

She shook her head. "He's two years younger than me, more like a kid brother than a cousin. He'd always run tame in our house…well, you've seen his father. Danny had problems enough of his own. I should have tried to keep him out of trouble. Instead…just before I turned seventeen, my mother remarried and I ran away from home. Danny went with me." Her voice caught. "That's when he started drinking."

"Your folks are divorced?" There was a tug, hard and specific, of understanding. He knew what divorce could do to kids.

"No, my father died when I was fourteen. My mother was devastated. Grief sent her inside herself, and I felt— oh, invisible. Wild with grief at first…my father and I had been close. You might say I didn't handle it well." Her smile caught and held this time. "*If* you were given to gross understatement."

"Fourteen is a rough age. You can't date or drive, but you aren't a kid, either. You don't have a clue what you want to be—other than not fourteen anymore."

Her eyes brightened with curiosity. "I have a hard time picturing you unsure of your goals, even at fourteen."

"I knew what I wanted to be. I also knew it wasn't a practical goal."

"Who told you it wasn't practical?" She sounded indignant on behalf of that long-gone boy.

"No one." Jacob was pleased. She was thinking of something other than her cousin now. Maybe he didn't know much about comforting, but he was distracting her. "I figured it out myself. I wanted to be a flying ace—a World War One flying ace. Or a member of the French Underground in the Second World War. Or a cavalry officer at the Battle of Waterloo."

She chuckled. "I have to agree—those weren't practical goals. Had a taste for blood, history and heroing, did you?"

"*Hero* isn't a verb."

"You know what I mean. You wanted to go back to times when we thought we knew who the good guys and the bad guys were. You wanted to be one of the good guys."

"Fourteen is the age for that sort of thing." He shifted, uncomfortable with talking about himself. "What did you want to be back then?"

"Aside from not-fourteen, you mean?" Her smile came easier now. "I'm afraid most of my goals were negative, centered around what I didn't want to be. Like a cheerleader or a model or a beauty queen."

His eyebrows lifted. "I'm no expert on teenage girls, but I seem to remember a number of them wanting those things."

"Maybe I would have, too, if my mother hadn't wanted them so much. She was always trying to talk me into entering a beauty contest." She chuckled. "To foil her, I tried to get a tattoo. Had it all picked out—a design with a snake and a rose that I considered terribly symbolic. I was all of fifteen then, and nuts about symbolism."

Humor and horror mingled. "Good God."

"Hey, it would have worked. You may not have noticed, but beauty queens never have tattoos on their faces."

"Now that you mention it, I've never seen a tattooed Miss America. I take it the operator of the tattoo parlor you chose wasn't crazy about, ah, defacing a minor."

"Defacing?" She pulled her lips into a frown, but the corners twitched to match the mirth in her eyes. "Bad, Jacob. Very bad. You're right, though. For some reason, the man who owned the place didn't believe I was eighteen."

Jacob looked at the soft cheeks colored once more by the warmth of her blood, and felt something soft and unnervingly tactile move inside him. As if he had touched her, when he hadn't. When he spoke, his voice was lower than he'd intended. Huskier. "It would have been a crime to mar such a face."

Darkness ghosted across her eyes, a hint of memory. Was she remembering the woods, the sound of water smoothing itself over rocks? The feel of his hands on her?

Or the feel of Ken Lawrence's fist?

She moved then, putting a couple of feet between them, stopping at a table to fiddle with the magazines, straightening them. "It would have been a crime to tattoo any girl that young," she said lightly. "Literally. Which is why I don't have a snake and a rose on my cheek today."

"I don't understand why you wanted to try. Even then, you would have been very beautiful. Were you so lacking in vanity?"

"Oh, I was vain enough." She straightened. "Competitive, too."

"But not about your looks."

"I didn't want to compete that way. It felt wrong. Winning a beauty contest wouldn't have meant anything, because I would have won for something I'd been given at birth, not something I'd done. Losing would have been just as bad, though." She grinned. "I hate losing. At anything."

"Sounds like you had a pretty clear set of priorities, even back then."

"Don't give me too much credit. At fifteen, I just knew the whole idea of beauty contests made my stomach hurt. I never could explain it to my mother."

Jacob was beginning to dislike her mother. "She pushed you?"

"Not like some mothers do. I mean, she accepted it when I refused—every time I refused. She'd get this sad look on her face, though." She shook her head. "The whole beauty

pageant thing didn't become important to her until after
Dad died. I look a lot like him, you see.''

He thought he was beginning to. Before he could decide
what to say, however, they were interrupted by her friend.

The sergeant moved those long, skinny legs of hers
briskly, and spoke the same way—to Jacob, not Claire.
''Claire's uncle is getting a cup of coffee. While he's out
of the way, I've got a couple questions for you.''

His eyebrows lifted. ''Ask.''

She gave him a long, appraising look, head to toe and
back again. Such a careful scrutiny might have been a
come-on. Jacob was double-dead sure this one wasn't. He
felt as if his assets—physical, mental and spiritual—had
been totted up and entered into the appropriate columns.
The assessment amused him. And reassured him. Claire
needed a friend like this one.

''She's been staying with you, I understand,'' Jackie
said.

''Yes.''

Her eyes were calm. Cop's eyes. Her body language was
pure challenge. ''What kind of security do you have at that
big house of yours?''

''Good enough that I plan to buy the company that
makes it.''

''You do, huh?'' She lofted one eyebrow at him. ''Don't
let her go anywhere alone.''

''I won't.'' He was grimly certain of that.

''Hey.'' Claire waved a hand between the two of them.
''I haven't turned invisible, have I? You two might try
talking to me, instead of around me.''

''All right.'' The sergeant's face split in a generous grin.
''Speaking directly to you—don't go anywhere alone. Sit
tight in this man's house behind that good security system,
and don't make me worry about you.''

"I don't think that's such a good idea."

Something all too similar to panic slithered in Jacob's gut, hot and unwanted. "You'll stay with me."

"There are three other people living in your house."

Her friend rolled her eyes. "This is a *good* thing. The more people around you, the better."

"Not if Ken's delusional. He doesn't care who he hurts. I shouldn't have taken the job in the first place. I shouldn't have gone to that party." She hugged her arms to her. "Ken's parents saw me with Jacob there. If they have any sense they won't say anything to Ken about it, but..."

Jacob grimaced. "But you can't count on that pair for sense."

"I know what Ken will think. What he thinks anytime I come within breathing distance of a man. I can't go back to Jacob's house. Ada might not be in danger, but there's Cosmo, Jacob's secretary. He lives there, too."

Jackie shook her head. "Where you going to go, then? Not back to your house. You aren't that stupid. But your mom's in California, and your uncle isn't an option."

"I...thought I might stay with you again."

"You know you're welcome, but he knows that's where you stayed last time. Besides, I'm gone more than I'm home."

"She'll stay with me," Jacob repeated. That slippery feeling was back, making his voice harsh. Lust, he decided. That was what had his gut twisting.

Claire slanted him a haughty look, duchess to peon. "I don't think so."

Her expression made him want to smile. Her stubbornness made him want to shake her. And his gut twisted tighter. "If you're worried about what happened earlier, don't. I'm not going to jump you."

"Ah..." She darted a quick glance at Jackie's interested

face. "That isn't the point. I won't put other people in danger."

"Just yourself? Are you going to stop going to the convenience store? And the grocery store, the gas station—everywhere there are other people?"

"I—that's different. Ken isn't some crazed sniper with a grudge against the world. He just..." It was barely visible, the slight shiver that broke into her words. But Jacob noticed it. "He's fixated on me, not the lunch crowd at McDonald's."

"We don't know what he'll do to get to you." He paused, letting that sink in. Maybe Lawrence was sane enough to avoid attacking her in public. If not, an old lady standing next to her in the checkout line at Furr's might be in as much danger as anyone she lived with. "I'm not exactly helpless, and have you looked at Cosmo? The man could bench-press a tank. You don't have to protect him. Or me."

She shook her head. "Unless you can grab bullets out of the air with your bare hands, you're just as vulnerable to a gun as anyone else. So is Cosmo."

"North can post some guards. Between them and the existing security systems, Lawrence won't get close enough to shoot anyone."

"Adam North?" Jackie asked, interested. At Jacob's nod she said, "He's good. Listen to this man, Claire. He's right. You're wrong."

"But—"

"But nothing. He's your boss, right?" Jackie's smile was sly. "For once, do what you're told."

Claire threw up a hand. "All right. All right—though you're enjoying this far too much, I agree. Once I've found Sheba, I'll go to Jacob's and stay there."

"You aren't going back to your house until Lawrence is behind bars," Jacob said. "I'll see that you get your cat."

"Jacob, I appreciate your willingness to shed blood for a good cause, but she won't let you touch her."

"I'm not going to pick her up. My brother is."

Her brows knit. "I thought Michael had left the city."

"My other brother. Luke. He could teach the Pied Piper how to charm beasts. I called him earlier and asked him to get your cat."

"The thing is, Sheba doesn't like men. Any men. I even have to take her to a female vet. I think some man must have mistreated her before I found her. She won't come to your brother, and if he finds her, she won't let him catch her."

"She'll like Luke." Animals and women all liked Luke. Especially the wounded ones. "It won't hurt to let him try."

"At least tell the poor man she's had all her shots," She started to pace, stopping near the door that read Hospital Personnel Only to frown up at the clock. "Do you think that thing is broken?"

Jacob didn't answer. Jackie did, but he didn't listen. Claire didn't need to know the correct time. She needed to know her cousin was going to be all right, and neither of them could tell her that.

He watched her resume her pacing, watched as she and the cop exchanged a few words—some kind of private joke, he guessed. It seemed to involve a coach they'd once had, and Claire's stubbornness. He watched her smile, her shoulders stiff and her face tight with fear, and give her friend a reassuring hug.

The hot, coiled feeling inside him wound tighter. "I won't let him get to you," he said suddenly.

She met his eyes. The shadows in hers were deep. "Ken

has put two men in the hospital because of me. If you've got any heroing urges left over from when you were fourteen, squelch them. You understand? That's the last thing I need.''

He nodded. He had no desire to play hero. He was just going to keep her safe. ''There's one other thing you'll need to consider. Later, though. Not tonight.''

She sighed. ''What's that?''

''I want you to marry me.''

Her jaw dropped. She was staring at him in utter, blind shock when the door behind her opened and a man with thinning hair, a ruddy complexion and blue scrubs stepped out.

''Ms. McGuire?'' he said.

The shock chilled on her face. She turned, and Jacob couldn't see her expression, only the rigid set of her back.

The surgeon smiled. ''Good news.''

Eight

Dallas was never truly quiet. Even at four in the morning, headlights still lined the Expressway, while other lights glowed in stores and on street corners to discourage vandals and prowlers. But the cars were fewer, and the houses were dark.

Claire watched the lights blur as they approached, turn singular and distinct as they passed, then vanish behind them. She was all but hypnotized by motion and weariness, yet she couldn't sleep. Her thoughts turned slowly in a gummy mass, one stuck to the next in no apparent order.

There was no wind in her face to force her awake. Jacob had put the top up before they left the hospital.

Jacob.

Once Danny was in recovery, she'd tried to get Jacob to go home. He'd ignored that. Pretty much the way she'd ignored his crazy proposal.

He hadn't mentioned it again, thank God. She didn't

want to deal with it, with him, with the kaleidoscopic confusion she felt every time she thought of it.

She couldn't stop thinking of it.

One other thing you'll need to consider, he'd said. *I want you to marry me.*

It was absurd. No one proposed in such a way, at such a time. In a hospital waiting room, for heaven's sake. With her cousin in surgery. And Jackie standing right there, eyes popping and mouth dropped open.

Claire would have liked to convince herself he hadn't meant it. That it had been some sort of bizarre joke, or an offer made impulsively out of concern, one he would be happy to forget. He hadn't mentioned it again, after all. But he *had* meant it. Her certainty on that score was almost as baffling as his blasted proposal. However little sense it made, Jacob West wanted to marry her.

But why? He didn't act like a man who thought he was in love. His offer to marry her had to rank in the top ten of the most *un*romantic proposals ever made. That *why* puzzled her into exhaustion, but her response to the ridiculous proposal was more than puzzling. It scared her spitless.

She closed her eyes and leaned her head against the headrest, but thought followed sticky thought, taking her where she didn't want to go.

"I'll love you forever." Ken had told her that the first night they met. She remembered his voice—a clear, true tenor that used to be raised in choir at his church. She remembered too much. Opening her eyes, she stared out at the blur of lights and the huddled dark houses.

She didn't want anyone in love with her, ever again. Friendship, caring—those lasted. Love was too much like insanity.

Ken Lawrence wasn't the only man who'd ever written his own needs and desires onto the template of her face, of course. But he was the only one who'd convinced her what he felt was real. She'd paid dearly for that mistake. So had others. Danny...

"Can't sleep?" Jacob asked.

His voice was deep and quiet in the darkness. It should have been soothing. It wasn't. "My mind's buzzing."

"The surgeon said your cousin's chances for a complete recovery are excellent."

The man had explained the surgery carefully, but the medical jargon had sheeted off her anxious mind like water, leaving little more than his assurance that Danny was alive, that no critical areas of the brain had been damaged, and that she could see Danny for a few minutes once he was out of recovery.

"He opened his eyes," she said. "When they let me in to see him. He opened his eyes, and he knew me." He'd been hooked up to all sorts of beeping and humming machines, his body thin and helpless beneath the sheet, his face bloodless as death. But he'd opened his eyes when she held his hand. He'd looked right at her and known she was there.

"That's a good sign."

Claire tried to hold on to the image of Danny's blue eyes, dazed by pain and drugs, but aware. Other worries nudged it away. Like the practical question of how she was going to pay that surgeon for his work. She'd put herself down as being responsible for the bill.

"How did you and the sergeant become friends, anyway?" Jacob asked, swinging off the interstate to the access road.

She seized the subject gladly. "Basketball. I tried out for the team in the eighth grade. My mother wanted me to be a cheerleader, but I didn't want to stand on the sidelines and cheer for other people." She smiled reminiscently.

"Jackie was about twenty times better than me—or anyone else. Not just because of her height, either. She's fast. She moves so smoothly you don't realize how fast she's going until the backwash hits. So, being hopelessly outclassed, naturally I spent most of that year trying to beat her."

He chuckled. "You did mention something about being competitive. That led to you becoming friends?"

"I can't take much credit for it. Jackie could see I wasn't much of a threat, bless her, so she never took the competition thing seriously. Lord, that used to tick me off. I was so intense back then. Jackie was, too, but not about basketball. Even then, she knew where she was going, what she wanted to be. A cop."

"You admire her."

"Of course."

"Eighth grade…that was the year your father died, wasn't it?"

Her smile faded. "Yes. It was."

He slowed and stopped at the last traffic light before reaching the West mansion…or manor. Or castle. Here, the houses were dark except for an occasional porch light, the streets echoingly empty.

"My mother died when I was five."

Startled, she swung her head to look at him. His face was limned by the dash lights, a harsh collection of angles that told her nothing. "That's terribly young to lose a parent."

"Yes. My situation was different from yours, of course. My parents were divorced, and I'd been living with my father since I was three."

Yes, his situation had been different. Jacob's mother had left him twice—once through the divorce, and again in the most final parting. "At any age, death feels like abandonment. At least at fourteen I knew that my father hadn't meant to leave me.''

The light changed. He flicked her an unreadable glance and accelerated smoothly. ''I wasn't looking for sympathy.''

''Sympathy and understanding aren't the same thing.''

''I did want you to understand. I don't believe in divorce when children are involved, not unless the situation is dangerous or unhealthy for the children.''

''Ah...''

''The possibility of children exists, however careful we might be.''

Her stomach hollowed—and her eyebrows snapped down. ''You're jumping to one hell of a conclusion.''

''I'm not assuming you'll marry me. I'm not assuming a blasted thing, which is why I want to discuss things like children and our respective attitudes about divorce. The last time I asked a woman to marry me, I thought I knew what she wanted from marriage. I was wrong.''

''The last time?'' she asked faintly.

''I had planned to marry a woman I knew well. Unfortunately she turned me down.''

A bubble of feeling rose quickly, and burst. Claire couldn't help it. She started laughing.

He frowned. ''I do seem to be amusing you regularly tonight.''

''I'm laughing at myself, not you.'' He hadn't fallen for her—not for her face, much less the person behind the face. No, he had, apparently, decided to get married, but love had nothing to do with his decision. This would teach her to jump to conclusions based on ego and...just ego, she told herself firmly. Nothing else could be involved. Not this fast.

''So I'm your second choice, am I? No, wait—don't answer that." She grinned. "If I was farther down the list than number two, I don't want to know."

"I don't have a list." He sounded irritated. "I have a reason for wanting to marry quickly, but I do not have a list of prospective brides."

"Just two of us, then." Her mirth was fading. "Jacob, I'm sorry I laughed. And I do appreciate the honor you've done me, but—"

"I'd rather you didn't give me an answer yet." He pulled into the long driveway that led to his house. "You've had a rough night. I hadn't intended to bring this up yet..." His voice drifted off in what might have been bafflement. "I spoke on impulse, but the offer is genuine."

"I suppose you were carried away by the emotion of the moment."

"You're still laughing." He reached up to hit the button that opened the garage door.

"If you knew what had been going through my mind..."

"You might try telling me."

"A lot of nonsense, that's all."

He didn't speak as they pulled up inside the huge garage. He didn't say a word while they got out of the car and started down the path that led to the house. The moon was down, and the world was four-in-the-morning cold and quiet.

When he did speak, he sounded disgusted. "My timing was lousy, wasn't it? You've got a crazy man stalking you. When I sprang that proposal on you, you were afraid I'd become fixated on you, too. You don't have to worry. I'm not Ken Lawrence."

"No, you're not." He was strong, whole where Ken had been shattered by forces Claire had never understood. And yet... "Ken proposed to me on our second date."

"Do you really think I'm like Lawrence, or do you need to keep reminding yourself of him for some reason?"

Maybe she did need to remember Ken, how believable he'd been. How much she'd *wanted* to believe in him. Claire sighed. As if she'd breathed out the last of the night's strength along with that breath, she wobbled between one step and the next.

His hand was there immediately, gripping her elbow, steadying her. "I've handled this poorly. We can talk in the morning."

"In the morning…" Discouragement and fear hit in equal measures. "In the morning, I'll have to give you my resignation." And go somewhere. Right now she had no idea where.

"You promised your friend you'd stay with me."

"That was before you proposed and I turned you down. That sort of thing doesn't make for a good working relationship."

"You haven't turned me down yet."

"Not for lack of trying," she said dryly.

"Even if you do decide not to marry me, you can't quit. I need you. And you need to stay here, where I can keep you safe."

Why? Why did he want to keep her safe? Why did he want to marry her? "I don't understand why you're doing this."

He kept his hand on her elbow as they stepped onto the flagstone patio. There were two back doors—one that opened onto the library, one to the kitchen. He steered her toward the library door. "Let's have a drink."

"What?" Surprise broke into a laugh. "Now?"

He unlocked the French door and tapped a code into the small box set high on the inside wall by the door. She shook her head as she followed him into the darkened library.

"Jacob, it's after four in the morning. I'm wiped out. I don't want to stay up and socialize."

"I don't think you'll be able to sleep until you've had some answers. Besides, you put away enough of the high-test sludge that passes for coffee at the hospital to keep you buzzing, however tired you are. A drink might help you relax."

It would be simple to be sensible. To tell him good-night and walk down the hall to her room, where she could pull off her clothes and fall into bed...alone.

She stayed. She wasn't sure why. There was something seductively pleasant about being alone with him in the sleeping house, the darkness softened by a single puddle of light from the wall sconce he'd switched on. Maybe she was too tired to move, drugged by events and exhaustion into an odd passivity. Walking away seemed as if it would take tremendous effort.

Yet she wasn't sleepy. Brain-dead and aching for rest, yes, but her mind kept turning over the same gummy thoughts.

Maybe a drink wasn't a bad idea, she thought when he approached her with a half-filled glass in each hand. It might lubricate those sticky thoughts, letting them slide right out of her head so she could sleep.

Or maybe she wanted a few more minutes with this baffling man.

She shook her head, trying to rouse the wariness she knew she ought to be feeling. "I really shouldn't."

"Scotch and water." He handed her one glass. "I hope that's okay."

The smoky aroma made her nose wrinkle. "I suppose. For medicinal purposes."

"Not a Scotch fancier, I take it."

"It was Ken's drink."

He glanced at the glass still in his hand. "Should I cultivate a taste for Irish whiskey?"

"It doesn't matter what my *employer* drinks." She took a sip. The taste was strong, not entirely unpleasant. Malt and smoke, medicine and memories…it was the memories that made her set the glass down on the nearest surface after that single taste.

"I'm glad you agree I'm still your employer." He put his own drink down, untasted, next to hers. "But I'd like to exchange that status for another. No," he said when she tried to interrupt. "Don't say anything yet. Give me a chance to present my case."

"We aren't in court." She shoved her hair back, her hand lingering on her nape to rub at the tension there. "But go ahead. I can't seem to stop you."

"First, don't even think of leaving here. Even if you decide you don't want me for a husband, you're better off here than somewhere Lawrence can get at you. You'll have my protection, Claire." His voice was low and intense. "No matter what you decide. But what happens in a month, when Sonia comes back?"

"I…" She hadn't thought that far ahead. Had carefully avoided thinking about it. "Jackie will have him in custody by then."

"Maybe. But she has to have evidence. If your cousin can't testify against Lawrence, what can she do? What will you do?"

What, indeed? "If I have to, I'll leave Dallas."

"And if he follows you?" He came closer. "Claire, the man has apparently nursed his obsession through six years of prison. If your friend can't put him away before Sonia comes back, what will you do?" He paused. "If you marry me, you'll have my protection for as long as you need it."

"Did it ever occur to you that I might not want to depend on someone else for protection?"

"Whether you want it or not, you need it. And what's wrong with that? Women have married for protection for centuries."

"Those would be the same centuries that women were treated as chattel, I believe."

Humor glimmered in his eyes. "All right. If not for protection, what about money? Also a historically common motive, one that remains popular today."

"Maybe with some women—or men. But it strikes me as a legalized form of prostitution."

"Only if you go to bed with me. Will you be easier to seduce if we're married?"

Her heart kicked, sending a quick, excited message to the rest of her body—which very much liked the idea of being seduced by Jacob. She ignored it. "Are you saying you wouldn't expect to have sex with your wife?"

The teasing smile vanished. "I'd expect nothing more than whatever you promised me. We can work out the terms ahead of time. Of course, some of it we might not want to put into writing." Again, that glint of amusement. "Like the part about whether you go to bed with me or not."

"Jacob." Sadness slipped inside her anger, softening it when she wanted to stay strong and angry. "Marriage isn't a merger. It isn't some sort of business deal."

"It can be."

"Only if one person is selling something to the other. I won't sell myself."

"Then marry me for Ada's sake."

"What?" Off balance, she placed her hand flat on the wall, as if she could steady her mind by catching herself physically. "What does Ada have to do with this?"

"You don't want to marry for money, but I do. I have to." His gaze, his entire concentration was focused entirely on her. As if, in that moment, nothing else existed for him. Only her.

Desire shivered over her. He shouldn't look at her that way. It was arousing and unfair, and she didn't want to become the object of a man's obsession. Not again, never again.

But her body itched with nerves. Awareness drew her skin tight, and longings she refused to acknowledge crawled out of their hiding places, making her move restlessly.

She turned her attention to the slightly stuffy elegance of the library instead of its owner. Walls of books encircled them, books bound in leather and hardback and paper. The wood of the shelves was old and dark, polished to a well-loved glow. In one corner, a globe the size of a baby elephant's head rested in an ornate brass stand. She moved over to it, gave it a spin, and watched the world turn, whirling and whirling on its brass axis. And going nowhere.

"You want to marry me for my money." She shook her head. "I hate to tell you this, but I'd bring more debts than capital to your proposed merger."

"You're talking about your cousin's hospital bill, aren't you? Well, if you marry me, you won't have to worry about that. I can take care of it. We'll put it in the prenuptial agreement."

Exasperated, she rubbed a hand over her face. "There's not going to *be* a prenuptial agreement. I turned you down, and you are not making any sense. None at all. Why would you even want to marry me? You don't know me, and I don't have money—"

"You've forgotten the trust."

The trust. The will, his father's will, that left his fortune to his sons. *After* they married. All of them. "Your marriage alone won't dissolve the trust."

"Luke and Michael will marry in the very near future. And so will I." He crossed to her, his pale gaze steady. "You, I hope."

"Why?" She meant to demand. The words came out breathless. "Why do you need money? Why would your brothers agree—"

"For Ada. She's got Timur's Syndrome. She'll die without regular treatments."

"Dear God." Stunned, she searched his face and found only determination. "Is she all right? Will she be all right?"

"If she gets the treatments, yes. Probably. But they are experimental—and expensive. To keep her alive for another five years will cost between two and five million dollars. We have to end the trust."

It was a good reason, a worthy reason, for him to marry. But it was his obligation, his choice, not hers. "Jacob, I can't. There must be someone you know who would understand, who wouldn't ask for more from marriage than…" Money. Protection. His large, strong body in her bed at night. "Ask one of them."

"I tried that, remember?" His hands kneaded her shoulders gently. Persuasively. "She turned me down."

She felt trapped, pinned by his eyes, by his needs, by the giddy response of her body to his nearness. Too confused to argue, she put her hands on his chest, unsure whether she was holding him away or inviting him closer. "Why me?"

He slid his hands up to her neck in a slow caress, cupping her face. "Because I want you."

The stab of disappointment was keen. A lot of men wanted her. "I'm sure there are other women you want."

''Not like this. You're beautiful, but that isn't…that wouldn't be enough.'' Some shade of feeling clouded his eyes. Not desire, though that was there. Confusion? Could he be as confused as she was? ''It doesn't matter.''

It did matter. It mattered very much. She opened her mouth to say so.

And he took it.

The taste of him was already familiar. Her willful body knew it, craved it, and held still beneath the slow assault of his mouth, while her heart quivered and her hands clenched into fists. His tongue painted her lips, forcing nothing, inviting everything. His hands spread wide on her shoulders, then slid down her back, pulling her gently, inexorably, up against him.

His big body was hard, hot with a man's heat, the muscles tight with hunger. And careful, oh-so-careful of her as he cradled her up against him. His mouth promised her that same care; his hands shaped promises along her spine, her ribs, her waist.

Her back was bare…except for his big, warm hands. They dressed it in shivers, and her flesh greedily soaked up heat and promises both. She shuddered, one slow roll of sensation wiping her mind free, empty, blank—and filling her. With him.

Her muscles went limp, stunned with pleasure. And something more. Something that sent her hands roaming over him, claiming his shoulders, his back, his throat, where she found a rhythm in the hollow vulnerability beneath his jaw. His heartbeat was sounding a challenge as crazy as the one pounding through her own body.

She hardly noticed when he scooped her closer, because that was what she wanted. She didn't think it strange when the world tilted and, a dizzy moment later, the weave of the carpet scraped against her back as he laid her down. That, too, was what she wanted.

Yet there was a second—one tiny, blurred rip in time— when she froze. The past had teeth, and they sunk into her when his body came down on top of hers. For that one sliver of a second, reality shuddered, and she couldn't move.

He knew. When he lifted his head, his eyes were heavy, the pupils pleasure-dark inside their pale rims of color. His jaw was tight with hunger. And his fingers traced an unbearably tender line along her cheek. "Claire?"

Uncertainty ghosted across his voice, unraveling something inside her that had been wound tight for a long, long time. She stared up at him, bewildered. "Jacob, I have to ask you something. I have to know."

"Ask."

"Are you in love with me?"

He went still. Nothing showed on his face, nothing at all, but she felt his battle in the taut muscles.

After a long, long moment, he spoke. "No."

Relief shivered through her, a sense of safety…and pain. He hadn't tumbled into some fantasy that could rule him and deceive them both. But it hurt. As much as she needed to hear him deny it, she would have believed him if he'd said yes instead of no…because she wanted him to love her.

His fingers were gentle on her face. "I care. And I won't hurt you, Claire. Not ever, not under any circumstances."

"I know." And she did. But how could she tell him it had been shame, not fear, that had oozed out of the past to mar the present? Shame for all her mistakes, past…and present.

She kissed him instead. She threaded her fingers into short, silky hair as dark as the heat pooling in her middle and pulled his head to hers. She slid her tongue into his mouth where it could dance with his, and felt his pulse leap—along with hers.

His hand palmed her breast. Her breath fractured. When he reached behind her neck to unfasten the buttons that held her dress up, she shifted to make that easy. When his mouth came down on her breast, licking, sanity rippled in the shock wave.

Lust was sure and swift, its ancient imperative washing her nearly mindless. Nearly, but not quite. In the midst of physical delight curled something darker, scarier. Stronger. Something that called to every reckless impulse she'd ever had, singing of power and surrender. She was coming apart beneath opposing needs—for safety, sanity, the responsible boundaries she'd learned in the past six years. And for leaping, naked and laughing, off the highest cliff she'd ever found.

Her body tensed beneath those splintering needs. Her hands raced over him, greedy and sure, while her heart dipped and dived in wild uncertainty. His name was a gasp of wonder or fear.

"Shh." His mouth came back to hers. He kissed her slowly, thoroughly, telling her they had all the time in the world to discover each other, insisting she was precious. Fragile. Safe.

She didn't believe it. Not when his hands trembled where they touched her. Not when this need was so huge and fierce. Was she fragile? She didn't think so. There was fear as well as passion in the frantic drumroll of her heart, but she could race past it, accept it, ignore it. Fear wasn't the problem. Jacob wouldn't hurt her, not physically. He had said so, both with words and with the wordless, leashed strength of his hands and body. She believed him.

There were other risks than the physical. But she was willing, even eager, to take those risks with Jacob.

But could she promise that she wouldn't hurt him?

Her hands faltered. Her kiss turned softer. She knew how to touch a man, but she was suddenly, blindingly, unsure how to touch Jacob. She tried to ask, with lips and tongue and fingers, what he wanted. What he needed. Asked him to be there with her, as hasty and hungry and frightened as she was.

The muscles of his chest jumped at her touch. At some point his shirt had become unbuttoned. The hot silk of his skin drew her. She discovered the small nest of hair in the center of his chest with something like gratitude. Ken's chest had been smooth, hairless.

His hips flexed, pressing his arousal against her hip. She reached for the zipper to his pants, but the shape of him distracted her. He was huge and hard and fascinating.

He groaned and pressed himself deeper into her palm.

Lost in fire and need, Jacob had room for only one thought: Claire was going to give herself to him.

It wasn't what he'd planned. He'd meant to seduce her, yes, but not yet. Not when his control hung by a thread that was shredding fast. He'd wanted to show her to know how good they could be together—but he'd meant to offer only a taste, holding back the main feast for their wedding night.

Logic had never seemed so unimportant. Claire was ready to give herself to him *now*. There was no way in heaven or hell he could refuse that gift. But he would be careful of it. Of her. He'd felt her falter. She'd been coming apart under his touch, all fire and need—then, without warning, she'd turned uncertain. Vulnerable. As if she might break at a single clumsy touch.

She had fears; he knew that. She hadn't told him about

them, and she would have to—he needed to know, to understand. But that could wait. What couldn't wait was making certain she wasn't afraid *now,* in his arms. The only
way to be sure of that was to stop what she was doing with
the questing warmth of her hand. Immediately. Before he
yanked her panties and his pants down and thrust inside
her. Hard.

He shuddered. "Easy," he murmured to one or the other
of them, and gently pulled her hand away. And began to
carefully, precisely, drive her out of her mind.

Her mouth was there, waiting for him. He kissed it,
licked it, then wandered down the line of her jaw to test
the pulse at her throat. It hammered out a mad triple-time
beat. Her hands reached for him again, nearly sending him
beyond sanity, so he took them in his, gripping them
tightly, holding on to her and to his control while his mouth
traveled slowly, leisurely, over her body.

Her breasts were so beautiful. He told her that with the
wash of his tongue, the gentle suction of his mouth. She
moaned. He shivered, and traced a damp line down the
center of her stomach.

The material of her dress was in the way. He needed to
dip his tongue into her belly button. He needed her naked,
entirely bare, so he let go of her hands to finish stripping
her.

She agreed by lifting her hips, letting him pull off her
dress. She lay there, passive and achingly beautiful, her
eyes smoldering hot, while he tugged off her panty hose,
too. And that was the last he knew of control.

Claire wanted him naked. She made that plain by the
way she ripped at his shirt and tugged down his zipper, her
hands moving so fast he couldn't catch them. Or maybe it
was his breath, his sanity, he couldn't catch. She'd had

enough of gentleness, of the careful easing into passion. She wanted it all, and she wanted it *now*.

They tumbled together, rolling on the carpet, bare to bare and breath to breath. Hands, lips, tongues tried to learn everything, all at once. Something got in their way—a table? His back crashed into that obstacle, and her leg. Something on the table rattled and fell. Neither of them knew or cared. Chests heaving, they ended up with him on top, her legs open, need pressed against need.

Her hips urged him *in*. Mindless, he obeyed, and found heat. Dampness. A perfect, snug fit. A surge of feeling beyond pleasure, beyond everything.

Claire.

With the last instant of will, he held himself still. "You'll marry me," he said fiercely.

"Jacob—"

"Say yes." He moved—out, then in again. "Say yes, Claire."

"Yes, Jacob, I need you, need—" Her hips moved and she clutched at him.

He wanted more. Wanted her to say yes again, to say she would marry him and know what she was agreeing to. He groaned and tried to hold still a moment, just one more moment... "Claire. Slow down."

"Dammit, Jacob," she said, her hips pushing at his. "We'll go slow later. Move!"

In the midst of danger and heat, a sudden wash of feelings flooded him, feelings so strong and right he could do nothing but grin—cocky, certain. Happy. And bend his head to kiss her.

She kissed him back, kissed him as if there had never been another man, as if she were giving him something no one had ever touched in her before. He fell into the kiss and the rhythm, the sweet slap of flesh against flesh, the ancient summons carrying them both. She chanted his name until there were no words left, only the hard, driving fusion of bodies taking them where they had to go.

For all the thundering inevitability of it, Jacob's climax took him by surprise—the huge fist of sensation, grabbing him and shaking a shout from his throat. He heard her cry out, knew she was there with him—and drove into her one last time.

His heart still hammered, his chest heaved. He was physically wrecked, and what he felt was peace. He lay sprawled on top of her, and knew he was too heavy, but couldn't remember how to move. Her hand stroked his shoulder and back, stilling gradually.

She'd stopped moving? The quick, irrational fear that he'd smothered her gave him the energy to roll onto his side, taking her with him. Her head found a natural pillow on his arm and she sighed, her body limp and warm and cuddle-close. After another eon or two, he found the strength to lift his hand and push her hair back, because he needed, badly, to see her face.

She was asleep.

Feelings squeezed him in a place achingly tender and unfamiliar. Claire trusted him. She'd fallen asleep in his arms. He wanted to lie there with her forever, guarding her sleep, soaking up these strange feelings. He wanted to wake her up and offer her promises—wild, unreasonable, impossible promises. But the sweat was drying on his skin, and the air was chilly. She would soon be cold.

He eased away carefully, then knelt to lift her. His Claire was no lightweight, and she was as limp as a soggy noodle. Picking her up from the floor was no easy task. He grunted and got it done. She rewarded him by snuggling her head against his shoulder and looping limp-noodle arms around his neck.

He felt as if he'd just won the best deal of his life.

Her eyes didn't open, but she smiled. He would have liked to carry her to his bed, but beneath her sleepy smile lay exhaustion. The skin beneath her eyes was bruised to a fragile violet. She'd had a hellish day and needed sleep, but if she were in his bed he would make love to her again. Control could only be trusted so far.

So he carried her down the hall to Sonia's room, laid her in that bed, and tugged the covers up around her. And started to stand.

Before he'd done more than shift his weight, her eyes blinked open. "Hey," she said, her voice as drowsy as her smile. "Where do you think you're going?"

"You need some sleep. We have a lot of decisions to make in the morning."

"Jacob." Her hand rose to touch his lips, tracing them gently. "You can't hold me to a promise made under duress...no matter how delicious that duress was."

"Yes," he said, and stood. "I can."

"I didn't agree to marry you. Not really."

Fear touched him in the place that had been aching and tender a few moments ago. His hands clenched into fists. Grimly, carefully, he loosened them. He wouldn't lose her. He couldn't. She was *right*. "Yes, you did. We'll talk in the morning. Good night, Claire."

Nine

Claire slept alone, but she didn't wake up that way. Eyes closed, she drifted from dream into wakefulness, gradually becoming aware of sunlight pressing against her eyelids and the warm, living weight on her chest.

And the purring, buzz-saw loud.

Sheba? Her eyes popped open. Sure enough, a huge mud-and-smoke-colored cat sprawled across her chest, eyes squinted to smug slits at having found and claimed her human. Automatically Claire reached up to pet the cat the way Sheba preferred—firmly along the top of the head, then behind the ears and under the jaw.

Obviously Jacob's brother was a sorcerer. He'd cast a spell on her cat. Just as obviously Jacob hadn't bothered to lock her door when he left her last night. He'd opened it today to let her cat join her.

Last night. Thoughts and feelings blurred through her—a shiver of memory, the fear-sharp tug of delight. He'd made love to her so carefully at first. So precisely. But sex wasn't meant to be precise. It was messy and exciting, nourishing and awkward. Claire sometimes thought of it as God's gentle joke on mankind, a powerful gift you couldn't receive without shedding clothes and dignity alike. A gift you could cut yourself on, leaving wounds that healed unevenly…or not at all. A gift she'd refused for the past six years.

That's all this was. The yearning she felt for his touch this morning, for the deep completion of his body, was the natural product of her too-long abstinence, nothing more.

And the vast confusion she felt, as if she'd stepped out over a chasm where she'd expected to find solid ground?

She'd said yes.

How had that happened, for heaven's sake? How could she have let it happen? Not the lovemaking. She knew only too well how that had come about, and her body warmed at the memory. But she'd said yes when he asked her to marry him. She'd let him leave last night without making it clear he had to accept her refusal.

Did she have to refuse him?

The thought was beguilingly, deceptively simple. But she knew better, dammit. She used to base far too much of her life on impulse and emotion. The pain of her own bad decisions hadn't been enough to teach her caution. The price others had paid for those decisions had.

No way was she going to give in to hormones and longing again. Maybe, at this moment, she did want someone to lean on. Someone to offer her sanctuary. It would pass.

And maybe she did want Jacob until her vision blurred. That, too, would pass. Infatuation always did. The cold wreckage it left in its wake had nearly ruined her life once. Surely she didn't need to learn that lesson a second time.

Impatient with herself, Claire moved eighteen pounds of

cat off her chest and sat up, giving Sheba a quick apology in the form of another chin scratch. She glanced at the clock—and her eyes widened. It was nearly eleven. Thank goodness it was Saturday and she didn't have to go to work.

Just to the hospital.

Oh God, Danny. How could she have forgotten?

Guilt smacked her hard, sending her scrambling to the office area to call the hospital. Only she didn't have to. There was a note taped to the banana-shaped receiver.

Danny is doing well, she read. *His condition was downgraded from serious to stable. The doctor said he was awake earlier and responded to questions. You can visit him this afternoon.*

The note wasn't signed, but she didn't need a signature to know who had left it where she was sure to see it. Her gaze flickered to the door between her office and Jacob's. Feelings gusted through her, soft and strong as wind—and just as hard to grasp. She closed her eyes.

What was she to do with such a man?

He'd proposed to her, and he'd seduced her. There was no other word for it, however much of an accomplice she'd been in her own seduction. She'd been achingly vulnerable last night, and he'd seduced her—not just into passion, but into agreeing to marry him. For his own purposes, which didn't include love.

He'd also arranged for her to have her cat, so she wouldn't worry. He'd called the hospital—again, so she wouldn't worry. And his purpose for marrying her was to save Ada's life.

He had been there for her. Both last night and this morning, he'd stood beside her, ready and supremely able to do whatever he could to help her, protect her.

Jacob was a good man, honorable and strong and kind. Mystifying at times, but she had to admit that only added to his appeal. She loved his sneaky sense of humor and the way he tried to take care of everyone around him. But she didn't actually love *him*. She couldn't, not this fast.

And he didn't love her.

You don't want love, remember? a sly interior voice pointed out.

Eventually she would want to love again, she told herself, hurrying back into the bedroom to grab some clothes. Maybe not now. Maybe not until she was sure she could love strongly and wisely. Marriage—real, long-term, committed love—wasn't for weaklings, and it only worked when two people had built a shared wealth of knowledge and memories. She would make it clear to Jacob. Gently, firmly, completely clear. She couldn't marry a man she didn't know very well. In the meantime, she'd better get herself into the shower. She was sticky in places she hadn't been sticky in a long time.

She was…oh, no. Realization struck with the force of a freight train. Claire stopped dead.

Jacob hadn't used a condom.

And she hadn't even noticed.

Making love without protection wasn't right or responsible…but making love with Jacob *had* been right. Heart-stopping, world-spinning right, as natural as breathing… and just as dangerous, just as full of potential disaster.

Life always was.

As quickly as that, confusion settled into simple certainty. Simple, but not easy. Not safe or sensible.

Love never was.

Jacob watched his brother move restlessly around the office, picking up a paperweight, putting it down, fiddling with the blinds, moving on to fiddle with something else.

Luke had always been difficult. Moody, though that wasn't the way the world saw him; that bright, restless charm of his kept others at a distance every bit as well as Jacob's icy reserve.

He was more than usually tense today. But then, so was Jacob, after what Luke had just told him. "I suppose I should wish you luck," Jacob said at last. "I'd rather knock you across the room."

That sparked a glint of genuine humor in Luke's eyes. "Oh, pound on me, by all means, if it will make you feel better."

"Maggie is a special woman."

"I agree." Luke shot him a hard look. "You don't think I'll be good for her."

"Do you?"

Luke gave a short, harsh laugh and scrubbed a hand over his hair. "Hell, no."

"If you cheat on her, I'll pound you into the ground."

For a moment, Luke stopped moving. "I promised her fidelity. You think I'm going to break that promise?"

Jacob hesitated a beat too long. He knew it, and saw his doubt reflected in the quick slap of hurt in his brother's eyes. "No. You don't break your promises. I think you feel something for her, but damned if I know what that is."

Luke's grin flashed. "What, you think I'm going to give you an excuse to hit me?"

"Dammit, if all you want is some playtime in bed—"

"I wouldn't have had to marry her for that. Now, what about you? I've done my bit, and I understand Michael is ready to do his—and that you've got another candidate picked out for Mrs. Jacob West."

Jacob picked up a pen and toyed with it, suddenly uncomfortable. "You've talked with Michael?"

"He called me before he went off to play in whatever

corner of the world he could find people willing to shoot at him.''

Jacob's mouth crooked up in spite of the stab of worry. Luke's irreverent summary of their brother's job was a little too apt. ''It could be worse. If he'd stayed on his original career path, he'd be getting shot at by people in this country. With badges.''

''Yeah. And maybe some without badges.''

The door to Claire's office swung open. ''Jacob, I need to talk—oh.'' She stopped several steps into his office, her eyes widening as she stared at Luke. ''I, uh, didn't realize you had someone with you.''

The sight of her gave him a rush of pleasure. She was wearing a slim black skirt and one of her snazzy jackets, this one the color of peaches. Every hair was in place. Her makeup was understated, flawless. And she was barefoot.

He smiled at her flustered expression and moved to her. ''Claire, I don't think you've met my brother Luke. Luke, this is Claire McGuire.''

''It's a pleasure to meet you, Claire.'' Luke's gaze slid over her, and his smile widened. ''Very much my pleasure. Tell me you aren't involved with my stuffy big brother.''

Jacob didn't like the way Luke was looking at her. He didn't like glancing from one perfect face to the other, and realizing how right they would look together—two stunningly beautiful people. He slipped an arm around her waist and pulled her up against his side. ''I asked Claire to marry me last night.''

She tilted her head and met his eyes. Hers were bright and knowing, thoroughly aware of what he was doing. And amused, dammit.

Luke grinned. ''Did you, now? You've always had good taste. Claire, come here and let me welcome you to the family properly.''

"I'm afraid you're premature," Claire said dryly. "So is Jacob. I haven't accepted."

"No, Michael was premature. I was two weeks late, which my mother never let me forget. Jacob, of course, was right on time. Except this once?" He raised one eyebrow. "Did you rush your fences, Jacob?"

"We're negotiating."

"Negotiating?" Luke laughed. "First time I've heard it called that."

Jacob felt a stirring at his nape. If he'd been a dog, his hackles would have been raised. "It's time someone taught you some manners."

Claire spoke to Luke as if Jacob hadn't said a word. "You're the magician who found my cat and coaxed her into coming with you, aren't you? I want to thank you for that. You don't seem to be bleeding anywhere."

"She was reluctant, but a lot of females are wary of strange men. Fortunately I discovered her weakness for ham."

"I suspect you're good at that sort of thing. Almost as good as you are at getting a rise out of your brother."

"I usually have to work a lot harder than this to ruffle Jacob's feathers. Maybe he's short on sleep this morning."

She grinned. "He is."

She might have intended to say something else. Jacob didn't give her a chance. His arm tightened around her. When she turned her face to his, surprised, he kissed her. Hard and fast.

The kiss was for him, because he needed to touch her, remind her of last night. But the dazed look in her eyes when he lifted his head pleased him. So, for a different reason, did the speculative expression on his brother's face.

"Guess I'd better be going," Luke said cheerfully.

"Oh—wait," Claire said. "Don't hurry off on my account. I, uh, can talk to Jacob later."

She was flustered again. He liked that. "Luke was about to leave anyway. I think we've said what we needed to say." He met Luke's eyes, his arm still around Claire's waist.

Luke nodded slowly. "Yeah, I think we have. I need to rescue Maggie. Ada has her pinned in the kitchen. Good to meet you, Claire. I'm sure I'll be seeing a lot more of you. Not as much of you as Jacob does, of course—"

"Luke." Jacob made the name a warning.

Unrepentant, Luke tossed them a last grin and a wave and headed for the door. Leaving them alone, in a room that was suddenly too silent. The silence got heavier when she pulled out of his arms and moved away.

"Did I make you uncomfortable?" he asked, low-voiced. "That little scene with Luke…" She had every reason to hate and fear a man's jealousy.

Her smile flickered as she traced her fingers across the pile of printouts on his desk. "I can tell the difference between a little sibling rivalry and insane delusions, Jacob."

Good. That was good, but it left him more baffled than ever. What did she want? What could he give her? Frustrated, he crossed to her and sought an answer that wouldn't require the difficulty of words. He took her in his arms and kissed her.

For one instant, she held herself back from him. Then, with a small sigh, she relaxed against him, her lips parting as her arms went around him.

Fire. He tasted it in her mouth, felt it leap from her body to his, a heat that he craved. Sexual heat, yes, but more than that. More…. He pulled his head away slowly, dipped back for one more taste, then folded her tightly in his arms. "You don't regret last night."

"No. Do you?"

"No." There was more he needed to say, but he needed words for the rest of it. Damned if he knew what those words were. *Where are your scars, Claire? I know they exist, but I can't find them without help. How can I keep from trampling on the places that hurt if I don't know where they are?* "Why haven't you been involved with anyone since you left Ken Lawrence?"

"What?" She pulled back. Then her eyes narrowed. "What makes you think I haven't been?"

He knew because it was in the report—the one he didn't want her to know about. He was appalled at the way he'd given himself away. "I'd rather not say."

"And I'd rather you did."

He had three choices. He could lie, he could refuse to answer, or he could tell her the truth. Refusing to answer wouldn't help—she'd know he was hiding something. If he told her the truth, though, she might change her mind about him. She might quit, walk out the door and never come back.

But he couldn't lie to her. He simply couldn't, though it made him cold inside. "I had North's agency investigate you."

Claire stared at him incredulously. He'd had her investigated? The irony of it struck her hard, and she had to turn away, moving to stand by the window. He'd done the sensible thing, the practical thing. A man forced to marry quickly, a man who planned to propose to a near-stranger, had a right to find out as much as he could first.

Only she didn't want sense. She didn't want reason, or facts. She wanted him to be as passionately, crazily confused as she was. And that was stupid, just plain stupid. Hadn't she learned anything? "Did my life make interesting reading?"

"I...the only way I knew to approach finding a bride quickly was the way I would handle a business deal. I needed facts."

"It's an unusual courting tactic." The day was bright, the light coming through the window winter-hard and brilliant. It hurt her eyes. Or something did, because they were stinging. "Tell me—if we did marry, would you feel free to have me investigated again if you needed facts?"

"No!" She heard his footsteps, whisper-quiet on the carpet, as he crossed to her. Then she felt the warmth of his hands on her shoulders. "I wouldn't do that. It's different between us now. More personal."

She turned around. "Marriage is pretty personal, all right. So is making love. Oh, Jacob." Her smile came out wobbly. "How can I blame you for being sensible? It's what I want to be."

"I wanted to know what to give you, what you wanted in a man." His eyes were intense, his voice low. "I thought I could find out from the report, but I keep guessing wrong. You'll have to tell me. What do you want, Claire?"

You. The thought was clear, when nothing else was. She laid her hand along his cheek, and swallowed. "I'm confused."

"Do you want this?" He brushed his lips across hers. His hands moved to her waist, pulling her closer, bending his head to nibble softly at her neck. His hands slid along her hips while his mouth teased her. "Is this what you need?"

Heat shivered over her, rich and restless. It felt like an answer—the quick tumble of sensation when his hands scooped lower, cupping her, the swift slide into yearning that made her stroke her body against his. He groaned. Pleasure, heady and drugging, claimed her as his mouth found hers again. For a moment, the kiss was enough of an answer.

For a moment. "It's what I want," she said, her voice unsteady as she sought to put a little space between them. Not too much, because she needed this, needed the feel of him against her. Her hands found a place on his chest where she could feel his heart pounding, pounding. Just like hers. "But I think that what I need is time. I need to be sure."

"I don't have a great deal of time."

"I know." If he didn't marry her, he would have to look for someone else. For Ada's sake. The thought triggered a quick clutch of panic—and greed. She didn't want him with anyone else. Ever. "That woman..."

His eyebrows drew down. "What woman?"

"The one you asked to marry you first. Before me. I need to know about her."

"She isn't important. Not anymore."

"She was important enough for you to ask her to marry you. This isn't negotiable, Jacob. What's her name? What is she like?"

He was obviously reluctant, but he answered. "Maggie Stewart—no, it's West now. I almost forgot. Luke married her four days ago."

She blinked. "That's weird."

His chuckle was so soft she felt it more than she heard it. "I guess it is. We aren't exactly the Waltons."

He didn't look upset. His body didn't feel upset, tense with pain or regrets. "How do you feel about Luke marrying her?"

"Worried. I don't think it will work out."

"But you don't...you aren't..." She took a deep breath and got it said. "Are you in love with her?"

"With Maggie?" His eyebrows climbed in obvious surprise. "No. I like her. I thought she would suit me, that I

might suit her. She didn't agree, thank God. *You* suit me."
He paused as if he was groping for words. "You're right
for me, Claire. I want to be right for you."

How could he melt her with those few words? She closed
her eyes and laid her head on his shoulder and held on.
"How much time can I have to think this over?"

He was silent for several moments. She didn't mind. She
thought she might like to stand here for an hour or a day,
just like this, with his arms around her. His cotton shirt was
crisp against her cheek, warm from the flesh beneath. He
smelled faintly of some minty cologne or aftershave. And
of Jacob.

"I can't give you a definite time," he said at last.
"Maybe a month. Maybe longer. It depends on whether
Murchison tries to weasel out of the deal. If he won't honor
his commitment, I'll have to either find another investor,
or come up with the money myself."

A month. Could she find any certainty, any rational reason to marry this man in a month? "All right."

He began rubbing her back. "I'll give you as much time
as I can." One hand moved to her side, then eased between
them to cup her breast. "But I'm hoping you'll still let me
court you." His thumb drifted across the tip of her breast.

"Jacob." Laughter bubbled up. "Is that what you're doing—courting me? When Luke was here, you called it negotiating."

The smile started in his eyes, filling them with lazy heat.
"I can think of a few other words to use. Will you sleep
in my bed, Claire?"

It was, somehow, the most incredibly erotic question
she'd ever heard. She shivered. And nodded.

He approved of her decision. He made that clear with
his hands, with his mouth, with the low rumble in his chest
when she ran her hands over him. He wanted her—wanted

her right there, in the office. Right now. Her jacket and blouse were unbuttoned before she came to her senses.

She was breathless when she pointed out that Ada might come in. Or Cosmo.

"Let him get his own girl," Jacob muttered, kissing his way down the slope of her breast.

His target was obvious, and she approved—breathlessly, urgently. But she grabbed his head in both hands, her fingers slipping in the short hair, stopping him. Because in another minute, she might not care who came in and found them. "Jacob. Not here. Not unless your office door has a lock."

"Dammit." He straightened and grabbed her hand, pulling her toward her office. "They won't come in your room if the door is closed. And there's a bed in there."

"So there is." She thought of how alarmed she'd been at the sight of that bed, and smiled.

He tugged her through the door, past her desk and all those plants, stopping at the bed she'd made such a short time before. His smile mixed mischief and sheer, masculine greed. "I've had some interesting thoughts about this bed. Let me show you."

"I've got a few thoughts of my own." She stretched up and nipped lightly at his lower lip. "One problem, though. I don't have any protection. And I don't want to take another chance like we did last night."

"Another chance…" His eyes widened. He tunneled a hand through the hair she'd already mussed thoroughly. "Oh, hell. I won't fail to protect you again." His voice dropped to a husky growl. "I promise, Claire. I'll take care of you."

She believed him. Even if she'd found it in her to doubt

the word of a man who never lied, his shock had told her the truth. He'd forgotten. Just like her. Last night he'd been carried beyond control and reason, just as she had been.

The knowledge thrilled her. And terrified her.

Ten

The next morning a florist's van tried to deliver a rose to Claire at the West mansion. One perfect rose, bloodred. No card.

North's man intercepted it, of course. Claire never saw the rose. But Jacob had seen her face when he told her about it.

"It was a kid who placed the order," Jackie said. She sat in one of the deep leather chairs in Jacob's office, those long skinny legs crossed at the ankles. "Paid cash. The florist remembered him, gave a decent description—not that it will help much. He was fifteen or sixteen, white, dark hair, baggy jeans, athletic shoes." She shook her head, disgusted. "Sounds like fifty percent of the sophomore student body."

"Maybe a boy placed the order, but it came from Ken." Claire's voice was low and taut. She wasn't sitting, hadn't been able to settle anywhere since the rose arrived. "The rose came from Ken."

"Yeah, it did, but proving it's another matter." Jackie stood. "We'll try to find the kid, see if he can tell us who paid him to order a rose for you, but I have to say, the odds aren't good."

Claire's face was composed, but Jacob could feel the effort she was making to hold on. To hold herself together. He couldn't stand it. "I suppose the Lawrences are sticking to their story."

"They're alibiing their son, yeah. And we haven't been able to place him elsewhere, and Danny doesn't remember the attack, so—"

"I know. I know you can't do anything more than what you've been doing." Claire spoke calmly, but too fast. "But Danny might remember more. The doctor said his memory of the attack could still come back."

Or it might not. Because he couldn't do anything else— and he had to do *something*—Jacob went to her and put his arm around her waist. "The doctor also said he's going to be okay, even if he never remembers any more. No signs of neurological damage."

She gifted him with a soft, swift smile. "I need to remember that, don't I?"

Claire's cousin had been awake for several hours yesterday—long enough to see her, talk to her, when Jacob took her to the hospital. Long enough to talk to the sergeant, too. But the last thing Danny remembered was turning on the TV after coming back from his meeting. He'd seemed almost as frustrated by his failure as Jacob was.

Jackie's expression turned speculative as she eyed the two of them. Then she grinned. "Well, they do say that even the darkest clouds have a silver lining. Guess I'd better be going.''

"Thanks for your time,'' Jacob said. "I'll walk you to the door.''

"I think I can find it by myself. You two get back to work—or whatever you've got in mind for the rest of the day.'' She smirked at them. "Have fun.''

"I think she's on to us,'' Claire murmured when her friend was gone.

"Does that bother you?''

Her surprise was quick and obvious. "No, of course not. Though I expect I'll get a phone call later, followed by a merciless interrogation.''

"I guess cops are born nosy.''

An imp of mischief danced in her eyes. She turned fully into Jacob's arms, looping her arms around his neck. "She'll want to know if you're good in bed.''

His hands moved lazily over her. "And what will you tell her?''

"Oh, that you're adequate.'' Her smile was impish. "I might add that on a scale of tingles to explosion, you're nuclear meltdown.''

"I melted you twice last night.'' He remembered the sudden, stunned shock on her face when he'd sent her crashing over the peak the first time, with his hands.

"So you did.'' Her smile widened. "Like I said, adequate.''

"I know a challenge when I hear one.'' Because he also remembered the way her face and her muscles had smoothed out after making love, going limp and easy, he ran his hands up her sides to tease the sides of he breasts.

He'd made her forget about Lawrence and fear and everything else for a while last night. He could do it again. He rubbed his thumb across her nipple, and felt it harden.

Her lashes lowered demurely. "Why, Mr. West. You do have eccentric ideas about what constitutes proper office behavior."

"I prefer to be on an informal footing with my staff. I think I mentioned that." He brushed her lips with his while his thumb teased the tip of her breast. "Especially when I'm about to do something highly informal to—"

The phone rang. She jolted slightly and started to move away.

He tightened his hold. "Ada will get it."

"She's at the grocery store."

"Cosmo, then."

"This is Sunday, remember? And, no, we can't just let it ring. Not after what we learned about Murchison this morning."

He grimaced. The information broker's report that he'd ordered through North had arrived early that morning, before the florist's van showed up. The information in it wasn't good. Laura Murchison had started playing "hide the money" months before her husband caught on, and she'd managed to tuck away enough that it was highly unlikely her husband would be able to meet his commitment on the Tristar deal.

Jacob had made some phone calls, putting feelers out for an investor to replace Murchison, but things were coming to a head quickly on the takeover. Chances were, he'd have to front the money himself. Not that he had two million sitting around. He'd have to get an increase on his line of credit…which would be easy enough if the trust was going to be dissolved.

He'd promised Claire a month to make her decision. He

wouldn't go back on that. But he was going to have to do some pretty fancy juggling over the next thirty days. "I suppose I'd better answer it." Frustrated, he turned her loose, stalked over to this desk and grabbed the receiver. "Yes?"

The man on the other end was one of the business contacts he'd called that morning. He tried to focus on the conversation, but it was difficult. Claire was moving restlessly, pacing to the window, staring outside.

She seemed to reach some decision. She moved quickly away from the window—and right out of the office. Heading for the front door, from the sound of it.

Jacob spoke quickly. "I'll have to get back to you, Charles." He tossed the phone on a chair and raced after her, catching her just this side of the front door. "Where the hell do you think you're going?"

Her eyebrows snapped down. "Out. For a walk. Right here on the grounds, under the noses of those men you hired."

The immediate tension eased out in a long breath. The fear remained. "Claire, the rose proves one thing. Lawrence knows where you are. You don't leave the house—not even to walk on the grounds—without me or Cosmo."

She shook her head. "You don't get it. You're the one who shouldn't leave the house alone. Ken has never threatened me."

"You're afraid of him."

"Oh, yes. But that's an emotional reaction, not a reasoned one. He's never hurt me physically, never threatened to."

"You don't call waving a gun in your face a threat?"

Her eyebrows lifted. "I suppose that little detail was in

your report on me? Never mind—of course it was. He scared me badly that night, yes. He was completely irrational. But he didn't hurt me physically. He wanted to kill the man he thought I'd been with, not me.''

"After he shot Warren, he came after you. If your friend hadn't shot him—''

"He probably would have shot her. Yes, I know. But I don't think, even then, that he intended to hurt me. He wanted to make me go with him, make me stay with him.''

Furious, alarmed, he dropped his hands and paced away. Had she loved Lawrence so much she still couldn't see him for what he was? "Good God, woman! The man abused you. He went after you with a gun—''

"Ken was never abusive. I would have left him a lot quicker if he had been. He didn't even have a temper. He was too...flat.''

He stopped, scowling. "What do you mean?''

"It's hard to describe. The man I thought I'd known drained away a little at a time into the black hole of his delusion. Eventually he didn't feel anything strongly, not anger nor happiness, nothing. Until the only thing he cared about was *me*.''

The last word had come out in a burst of naked emotion. The fear was there—trapped behind her eyes, quivering in the unsteady hand that brushed her hair back.

She turned away, her head down so that the fall of shiny hair screened her face. "Of course, that was obsession, not love. But his feelings seemed genuine. Maybe they were, at first. He changed so much. So much.''

Jacob had a sick, hollow feeling. "You loved him.''

"Or thought I did.'' She swung into motion again, reminding him of Luke with her restlessness. "I wanted to help him. If he'd turned vicious, if I'd had any idea I was in danger—but he never threatened me. Even when I tried to leave him." Her laugh held no amusement. "He was devoted to me."

He selected his words as carefully as if he were wading through a minefield. "Most women would find that appealing."

"It was. At first. He was so romantic, so sure of himself...but that was part of his condition, that tremendous confidence." She paused, finding the strength from somewhere to smile with dark amusement. "His self-assurance was not exactly reality-based, as my therapist used to say. You know about that, too. I suppose. That I saw a therapist for a couple of months before the trial."

He felt the urge to apologize again. "I didn't see any of your therapist's records. North asked if I wanted them. I told him no."

"That's something, I guess."

For a long moment, she fell silent. Sunshine streamed through the window to set her hair ablaze; she stood straight and strong beneath the weight of her memories, her posture stating clearly that she wasn't interested in pity. Yet something about the graceful line of her spine struck him as fragile. Breakable, in spite of her strength.

"He used to reason with me," she said abruptly.

The sick feeling grew worse. "About what?"

"My men. All the men he was convinced were my lovers. He thought that I was the one with the problem, you see. That I was some kind of nymphomaniac, only I didn't remember the things I did. He'd explain it to me carefully, how I blocked out the memories because I felt guilty for betraying him. He was so gentle, so reasonable...and determined, utterly determined, to *help* me."

She tilted her face up. Her skin looked shocky-pale next

to the bright clamor of her hair. "I'm sorry. You don't want to hear all this—the long, sad story of my love affair with a madman. I know better than to dump all this on you, I just—"

"No." He couldn't keep himself from going to her, taking her hand. "For God's sake, don't apologize. You're right. I hate hearing this. I hate it because it hurts you, but I need to know, to understand."

Her hand trembled, then closed around his. "More facts, Jacob?"

He lifted their joined hands and kissed her knuckles. "I want to help. I don't know how."

"You've helped." She turned to him, put her arms around him. "You're still helping."

"I'm glad." He stroked her hair, offering what comfort he could.

But Jacob wasn't comforted.

He had thought Claire wanted reason and control from him. She didn't. Lawrence had reasoned with her, and she shuddered even now, six years later, when she remembered it. As for his control—he lost it. Every time he put his hands on her, he acted like a man drunk with passion, blind with his need for her. She seemed to like that, judging by the way she responded. But sex alone wouldn't bind her to him. He needed more.

Of course, she still needed Jacob's protection. That much, he could and would gladly give her, but sooner or later, Ken Lawrence would be stopped, locked away again. Then what? He wanted—badly—to marry her, but even that wouldn't be enough. Jacob knew only too well how temporary those vows could be. What he could give her to make her want to stay?

He couldn't think of a damned thing.

Late that night, Claire woke to the peaceful sound of rain on the roof…and the feel of an empty bed beside her.

Jacob's bed. It wasn't supposed to be empty. She opened her eyes and saw him standing near the window. His naked body was a lighter shade of darkness against the rain-blackened night. He looked strong, unreachable.

Then lightning lit the clouds and the night—and his face. And she saw the sorrow there, old and deep.

She tossed back the covers and eased out of bed.

He didn't turn. "Go back to bed, Claire. I didn't mean to wake you."

She padded over to him and put her arms around him. His flesh was chilled. He'd been standing here for some time. "What's wrong?"

"Nothing." His hand, smoothing down her back to her bottom, may have been meant as a distraction.

"Are you worried about the Tristar deal?" He was in a serious bind, and she knew it. She ought to either agree to marry him, or release him to find someone else.

She couldn't do either one.

"No. Quit worrying." He drifted his hand around the curve of one cheek, his fingers light and teasing.

She shivered, and it had nothing to do with the cold night air. "I will if you will." She looped her arms around his neck. "You're supposed to be a puddle of limp goo, you know. After the meltdown practice we put in earlier, you should be. So how come you aren't sleeping the sleep of the exhausted?"

"Limp goo?" He smiled. "As opposed to strong, manly goo?"

He made her smile. She couldn't help it, but she wasn't going to let him distract her, either. "Something is bothering you.'' She touched his cheek. ''Can't you tell me what it is?'

He looked away. ''It's the rain. I've always hated rain.''

''Why?''

He didn't answer for so long she thought he wasn't going to. When he did speak, his voice was so low she wouldn't have been able to hear him if she hadn't been standing so close. ''It was raining the day my mother died. I was waiting for her, waiting by the window. Watching the rain. She was late, and I was mad at her.''

She swallowed. ''Jacob.''

''We were supposed to go to Six Flags, but it was raining and she was late, and I knew I was going to miss out on what we'd planned. But still I waited…when someone finally came, it was in a police car.''

She closed her eyes and held him tightly. He'd trusted her. With a memory, a sliver of himself that went all the way down. Her voice, when she spoke, wasn't steady. ''The police came to the door when my father died, too. I remember it so well…''

''It isn't the sort of thing you can forget.'' He stroked her hair.

She wanted to comfort him, but he was comforting her. ''One of the policemen was so young, he had a pimple on his chin. I remember that, and the smell of the pot roast my mother had fixed for dinner. I still can't stand the smell of pot roast.'' She remembered, too, the searing, total disbelief. ''I was so sure they had the wrong house, the wrong family. That it couldn't really be my father who had died.''

He rested his cheek on the side of her head. ''I couldn't believe it at first, either. Maybe if they'd let me go to the funeral, it would have sunk in…I waited for her the next weekend, and the next. I think I had it fixed in my head somehow that I'd gotten the wrong weekend, that she'd come if I just waited patiently. Finally Ada noticed how much time I was spending by the window on Saturdays, and had a talk with me.'' He shook his head slightly. ''Not too bright, was I?''

Oh God. She wanted to go back and hug the small boy he had been, but all she could do was hold on to the man he was now. ''You were only five.''

Neither of them spoke for a while. They stood beside the window, arms and bodies loosely joined, and watched rain smearing the glass. The air was cold. Every part of her he wasn't touching grew chilly, and she shivered.

Jacob stirred. ''You're cold. I should have made you climb back in bed right away.''

''Not without you, tough guy. You're cold, too, even if you haven't noticed.''

He smiled and went with her, and when they lay together, their shared warmth made a cozy nest in the covers. Claire felt drained and sleepy and oddly happy. He was relaxed now, his big body loose and calm, cuddling her. And suddenly, answers were easy, and obvious.

She loved him. She was good for him, or could be. Claire smiled and touched the soft ends of his hair. ''Jacob? The answer is yes.''

He went taut again, still. Waiting.

Now her heart pounded. Now, she felt the edge she'd slipped quietly beyond between one beat of her heart and the next, and the dizzy whoosh of the wind as she fell. ''Yes,'' she said again, breathless with speed and certainty. ''I'll marry you. If you still want me.''

''Claire.'' His arms tightened, bruise-hard. ''Claire, you won't regret this. I'll make sure of that.'' He kissed her, slow and thorough. ''We'll pick out rings tomorrow.''

"Diamonds," Jacob announced—then, belatedly, glanced at Claire. "If that's all right with you?"

She nodded. At some point between parking in the dim, chill light of a late winter afternoon and walking inside the equally chilly elegance of the jewelry store, she seemed to have lost the power of speech.

The dapper little jeweler smiled. "Diamonds are always an excellent choice. If you would follow me—?"

Martin's, the small brass placard in the window of the store read. The carpet here was thick, the lighting subdued, the crystal placed on casual display emphatically art, not commerce. It was the sort of place that would never dream of sowing price tags among the merchandise.

The lack of those little white stickers made Claire nervous.

Jacob, on the other hand, was entirely at ease. He seemed to regard this trip to select their rings as a pleasant break in the real business of the day. She didn't know why his relaxed attitude irritated her, but it did.

"I didn't speak too quickly, did I?" he asked, low-voiced. "You can have whatever you want."

She managed a smile. "I like pretty, shiny things. Diamonds certainly qualify."

"Good." He tucked her hand in his arm. "I have an urge to dress you in diamonds. Diamonds...and skin."

Her heartbeat picked up. She felt the pulse of it in a place she wasn't supposed to notice in public. "Don't let me trip," she said lightly as they followed the jeweler across the thick, snowy carpet. "I'm afraid I'll turn an ankle. I don't think they've mowed in here lately."

He chuckled. "Martin can be pretentious, but he does know his stones. We'll find you something pretty and shiny."

And expensive, she added silently. But then, once she married him and the trust was dissolved, Jacob would be a very rich man. He could afford the best.

They were being waited on by the owner himself. Martin had waved his assistant aside when Jacob entered, obviously recognizing a valued customer. Jacob steered her to a niche with two plush chairs where Martin waited behind the nearby counter. The jeweler's head was bald and slightly damp, as shiny as the stones displayed in the case where he awaited them.

Claire's palms were damp, too. She wiped them surreptitiously on the linen of her skirt as she seated herself and wondered if she'd lost her mind. What had seemed clear and necessary last night was looking more and more like lunacy this afternoon.

"White gold or yellow?" Martin asked. "I do have a few pieces in platinum, but the selection isn't good, not in the already-set rings. You did say you wanted something immediately?" He glanced at Jacob.

They were to be married next weekend.

"Yellow gold," Claire said as firmly as if her mind weren't whirling with doubts. Then she glanced at Jacob, her eyebrows lifting in delicate humor. "If that's all right with you?"

The glint in his eyes said he recognized and appreciated her small joke. "Of course. It's your ring."

"Won't you wear one, too?"

"I—" He blinked, startled. "Yes, of course."

It obviously hadn't occurred to him. Claire put a hand on her stomach, where the doubts seemed to be lodged at the moment.

"A double-band ceremony," the jeweler murmured. "Lovely. It does limit us slightly, but yellow gold and diamonds…'' He bent and unlocked one of the cabinets. ''Yes, we have a nice selection. What sort of setting? Simple, ornate—perhaps something a touch avant garde?''

''Not avant garde,'' Jacob said, then smiled at Claire. ''Sorry. I need to let you answer once in a while, don't I?''

''I like simple styles.'' She thought about Jacob's hundred-year-old house and fifty-year-old convertible. ''Maybe a little old-fashioned.''

So what if Jacob hadn't planned to wear a ring? He'd agreed once she'd brought it up. He was willing to compromise, and that was important in marriage. He wasn't forcing anything on her. She'd said yes of her own free will.

But she hadn't expected to be rushed to the altar in seven days.

''And your sizes are—?''

''Six,'' Claire said. He was so alone. Did he even know how much he wanted people around him? That he wanted, craved, family? He'd kept that big old house when his brothers moved out. He'd gathered people to live in it with him—Ada and Cosmo and Sonia. Ada would stay—if she lived. Sonia would retire soon, and Cosmo already had plans to move out, to own a gym. And Jacob would help him do that.

Claire wanted to be the one who stayed. Forever. And the very thought of it had her heartbeat spiking in terror, and she didn't know why.

Martin set a small tray of rings reverently in front of them. ''I have a stone in mind I think will be perfect. Rather large, but exquisitely simple.''

She made a vague sound of agreement.

Jacob was marrying her for money, not love, of course. Money, and the undeniable passion that flared between them. He wasn't thinking of forever. Only three nights ago, she'd actually been relieved to learn that he didn't love her. How could so much change so quickly?

"If you would hold out your hand?"

She hardly noticed as the jeweler slipped a ring on.

Last night, saying yes had been easy. She loved him. He needed her. Given time, he might well come to love her, and last night, in the private darkness they'd shared, answers had formed and flowed easily. Now, in the light of day, nothing seemed easy. Claire's hand closed tightly.

"The ring is not to your taste?" Martin asked.

"Oh, ah…it's very nice."

"Nice." Martin's voice was carefully uninflected. "Yes, this is quite a nice stone. Two point six carats, and flawless."

The diamond was gorgeous. It was also huge, even bigger than the diamond earrings Ada wore to clean house…those gorgeous, gaudy trinkets that Jacob must have spent a fortune on.

He *was* capable of love, of the most extravagant sort. Just look at what he was doing for Ada, what he planned to do to help Cosmo.

"Do you want something larger?" Jacob asked. "A different cut or setting?"

"If the diamond was any bigger I'd have to start working out with Cosmo before I could lift it. It's a beautiful ring. I just…" She turned to look at him. His eyes were frowning, intent. He wasn't taking this business of getting a ring—of getting married—as lightly as it seemed.

Suddenly she knew what she wanted. She laid a hand on his arm. "Would you mind if we skipped the engagement ring and just got plain gold bands? Matching bands?"

"If that's what you prefer." He spoke casually, but be-

neath the crisp cotton of his shirt the muscles in his arm
tightened. "I did rather like the idea of you wearing my
ring."

How did she explain a purely emotional decision? "The
wedding rings stand for the real promises we'll make.
They're what count. An engagement ring—well, it seems
like a promise to make a promise. As if I were hedging my
bets, leaving room to change my mind." Her fingers closed
on his arm as she willed him to understand. "I'm not."

For a long moment he said nothing, and nothing showed
on his face—except the intensity with which he studied
hers. Then the muscles beneath her hand relaxed, and a
smile lightened his eyes. "Plain gold bands it is, then.
Though I hope you'll still let me buy you a diamond." His
voice dropped, turning husky. Intimate. "One you can
model for me. Later."

Heat rose in her cheeks…and elsewhere. She nodded.

Martin, to give him credit, didn't turn a single one of his
remaining hairs at the prospect of losing such a lucrative
sale. He showed them several sets of matching bands with
the same care and courtesy as he'd offered the huge diamond. He did perk up noticeably when, after they'd selected a pair of rings in heavy gold, Jacob asked to see
some necklaces. "Something shiny," he said. "And special."

Claire left the store with a diamond necklace tucked into
her purse and hope lifting her heart.

Loving Jacob was a risk, but it was one her heart had
already taken. Marrying him was an even bigger gamble.
It was no wonder nerves kept playing jump-rope with
doubts in her stomach. He didn't love her now, but she
mattered to him. He might come to love her in time. He
wasn't like her—emotional and impulsive and still, to her

shock, capable of tangling herself up in hopelessly romantic longings.

He was eminently worthy of being loved. He *needed* to be loved—just as he would need time to trust, time to grow into love. He wasn't a man who could tumble willy-nilly into the delicious, frightening place she found herself. She accepted that.

But it was scary, being here alone.

Eleven

Everything was working out, Jacob told himself as he set-tled behind the wheel. Claire was promised to him now, even if she wouldn't wear his ring until after the wedding.

She'd been awfully damned quiet this afternoon, though.

She wasn't sure of him yet. He wasn't fooling himself about that, and pushing her into a sudden marriage wasn't the best way to handle things. He ought to give her time to adjust, to trust him more. But he couldn't. If he gave her time, she might change her mind. Ken Lawrence would be locked away, and once the danger was past, what would Claire need him for?

But he would have to be careful, very careful, not to push too hard. Claire had loved another man once. She'd given herself to that man, promised to marry him, but it hadn't been enough. Nothing would have been enough, of course. Lawrence had been flawed, sick. In his sickness, he'd tried to force Claire to stay with him.

Jacob didn't want to remind her of Ken Lawrence. Ever. But he wanted, badly, to make Claire stay.

He'd driven the Chrysler today, wanted the comfort for her, the power for himself. The leather seats were sticky-hot from the sun. He switched on the air conditioning and hunted for a way to get Claire talking to him again. "Why don't we swing by the hospital and see if your cousin is awake?"

She flashed him a smile. "I'd like that. Thank you."

It was perverse of him to be annoyed by her gratitude, and foolish to be alarmed when she fell silent again. Her troubled expression didn't mean she was changing her mind about him. She had plenty of other things to worry about.

Her hands fiddled restlessly with a button on her jacket. "Jacob, about the wedding…"

Something cold and sharp sliced into him. "Yes?"

She sighed, and her hands stilled. "I just wish Danny could be there. Even if he's been released from the hospital by next weekend, he won't be strong. He may not be able to attend."

"I've been thinking about that. Danny shouldn't be alone when he's released, whenever that is. He should stay with us for a while, whether he's up to attending our wedding or not."

She reached for his hand and squeezed it. "Thank you. I'd been worried about that, but I didn't like to…I didn't feel I could burden you with a houseguest in need of medical attention."

"We're not roommates," he said curtly. "We're getting married. It's going to be your house, too." Because his anger was too sharp, he took a moment to smooth out his voice. "Has your mother called back to let you know if she'll be able to make it here for the wedding?"

"Oh, she'll be there. You couldn't keep her away. My

stepdad, too. Mom says Carl wants to give me away. I'm glad. Maybe it will finish healing the rift I caused when I was a mad, bad and crazy teenager.''

"You weren't all that bad. Crazy, maybe. After what you said about the tattoo you almost got, I'd have to agree with that.'' He hesitated. ''Was your mother upset when you called to break the news?''

She chuckled. ''She hit a ten on the shock scale when I first told her, but she bounced back. Her main regret is that she can't be here to drive us both crazy planning a huge wedding.''

"Looks like Cosmo will handle that for her. He's been pestering me with questions all afternoon. Do you mind him taking over?''

When they had told Ada and Cosmo they were getting married, Cosmo had been first astounded, then dramatically grieved that Jacob was ''stealing the finest flower in the city'' out from under his nose. And then he'd thrown himself enthusiastically into planning the wedding. Ada had slid Jacob a single, narrow-eyed glance and promised to have a talk with him later.

"Not a bit,'' she said cheerfully. ''Though I'm glad I talked him out of the doves. Did Ada manage to get you alone for that talk?''

"Not yet,'' he said grimly. It was only a matter of time, however. ''I'm not planning to tell her why I'm marrying, but she'll figure it out when the trust is dissolved.''

"She won't like what you and your brothers are doing for her?''

"Ada is the most cussedly independent female on the face of this planet. She hadn't planned to let me know she was ill, much less accept any help. I guess she thought it would be time enough for me to learn about her condition when she didn't wake up some morning.'' Anger and remembered fear knotted his gut. "I found her collapsed on the stairs instead."

"She did accept your help in the end, though."

"Not exactly." He glanced at Claire. "She agreed to let me set things up and fly her to the institute for treatment, but she doesn't know I paid for everything, or how much it cost. I want to keep it that way."

"But—can you do that?"

"I told her the insurance covered most of it, and she assumes her savings took care of the rest. I manage her savings and retirement money," he added. "I took some out of her savings and sent it to Varens—enough to cover what she thinks was the deductible."

"Jacob." She seemed to be struggling with some emotion. "Jacob, I think you should tell her. Maybe she won't like accepting help, but—"

"No." His fingers tightened on the steering wheel. "If she finds out, she's likely to refuse to go back for another treatment."

"Oh, surely not! And it would make her feel so good to know how you—all of you—feel about her."

"Ada is not a sentimental woman. She knows we care."

"Even a woman who isn't openly sentimental wants to feel loved," she said quietly.

"You don't understand." He struggled to find a way to explain without revealing things he had no right to speak of. "When I was young, my father made it—difficult—for her to work in that house. But she wouldn't leave. First she stayed for my sake, later because of Luke and Michael, too. But she had to be tough, emotionally tough, to survive. She's family, yet she isn't."

"It's hard for a woman to devote herself to raising other women's children."

Her perception triggered a memory he wasn't expecting.

The words came out before he had time to think. "He fired her once."

"Your father?"

"Yes." Twenty-five years later, the anger was still there. "After everything Ada had given up for us, the son of a bitch fired her in a fit of temper." He shrugged, trying to diminish the power of the memory. "We got her back, of course. But she always knew it could happen again. She stayed with us, but she had to protect herself. Ada can't stand to be dependent on anyone."

Claire was silent a moment. "Love, understanding and acceptance…those are pretty powerful gifts. I think I envy Ada."

Jacob's brows pinched together in an uneasy frown. She kept harping on love. He didn't trust that slippery word; his father had been "in love" with every one of his wives. "I've been talking too much. For blocks, I guess, since we seem to have arrived."

The hospital was a multistory building that had grown precipitously over the past decade, taking over the entire block it rested on. Late-afternoon sun painted the rows of windows a hard gold and stretched shadows behind the live oaks that flanked the parking lot in the next block. Jacob finally found a space near the west end of the lot. He pulled into it, but didn't cut off the engine.

"Look, if your cousin hasn't been released by next Saturday, we can have the wedding here," he said abruptly. "In his room, in the chapel, whatever."

"You wanted to be married at your home. And Cosmo has already arranged—"

"It isn't Cosmo's wedding." He looked at her. "I've never been married before. I'm not sure how to go about it, but I want to do it right. If what's right for you is having your cousin at the wedding, we'll work it out so he can be.''

A smile broke over her face. She unclicked her seat belt, stretched across the bench seat and kissed him.

Her taste, the pressure of her lips, were already familiar, as was the quick rush of heat. Familiar, yet still a surprise.

He'd barely begun to return the kiss when she pulled back. Her fingers lingered at his nape, teasing his hair. He wanted her to keep touching him. He wanted to pull her closer and kiss her smiling mouth.

"You're a good man, Jacob," she said softly. "Thank you. We'll see what Danny's doctor says before we decide, okay?"

It was going to work out, he thought as he climbed out of the car, optimism rising to make his steps light. She wanted him, and he thought she liked him, too. And for now, at least, she needed him. That was enough to build on.

Claire didn't wait for him to get her door. She rounded the back of the car, her purse hugged tight to her side. "I'm not used to carrying diamonds around," she said when she joined him. "Maybe we should have run by the house first to put the necklace up."

He took her hand. "You could wear the necklace if carrying it makes you nervous."

"Oh, no." Her smile was part mischief, part seduction. "The first time I wear the diamonds you gave me is going to be for you…privately."

As quickly as that, anticipation kicked up into need. One kiss, he thought—just one, to take the edge off. He stopped, tilting her face up to his with the knuckles of one hand while the other still held hers. Her lips smiled; her eyes turned smoky with desire.

He bent and brushed her lips with his, teasing them both.

Smiling as he did it. Then he flicked his tongue over her lips. Once. Her breath caught. Twice.

Her purse fell on his shoe.

She laughed, a little shaky. "See what you do to me? I'd better get it. Don't want to leave diamonds sitting on the ground." She bent.

And over her back, he saw a man in a dark gray suit walking toward them. He had sandy-brown hair, a sunny smile on his good-looking face—and a gun in his hand.

One second Claire was bending down to pick up her purse. The next, she was flat on the ground with a ton of solid male on top of her—and the hard crack of a gunshot echoing in her ears.

She found the breath to gasp—and he rolled them both over. Her shoulder bumped into a tire. His hands on her shoulders shoved her away from the tire. "Get under the car."

She didn't think, she just moved. Twisting, she wormed her way beneath the Chrysler's chassis. Heat radiated up from the pavement, down from the car. Her rump brushed some stinging-hot part of the car's underside and her breath jerked in her chest, dragging in metal-tainted air and terror.

"Keep going." Jacob was with her, somehow wedging his larger body between concrete and metal, too.

"Claire!"

The voice was horribly familiar, horribly close. She wriggled frantically away from that voice.

"Claire, don't run from me. Please—" Ken's voice broke. "Don't run anymore."

She reached the edge of the car and dragged herself out, crouching to tug at Jacob. He was still flat on his stomach, his lower body beneath the car, when Ken came around the rear of the car. Smiling.

Terror jammed in her throat. She tried to push Jacob back under the car, back to safety. He didn't so much as resist her efforts as ignore them, shoving himself out and onto his feet in one quick move.

In front of her. Damn him, he'd put himself between her and Ken. She tried to move out from behind him. He wouldn't let her.

"Claire. Oh, Claire, I've missed you. I love you so much." Ken's eyes were damp, shining with happiness. His gun pointed at Jacob, yet it was Claire he looked at, as if the other man weren't there. "Nothing has been right without you."

Jacob shifted, trapping her between the car and his body. "You need to put the gun down," he said, his voice surprisingly gentle. "You're frightening Claire."

Neither Ken's gaze nor his gun shifted. "You have to come with me. My parents aren't happy with me right now. They think I should move away, but I can't go without you." His eyes glowed with confidence and cunning. "Where do you want to go, Claire? The South Seas? Europe?"

"Wherever you like." Her voice cracked.

"Wherever we go, it will be paradise because we'll be together. Just the two of us." His voice grew dreamy. "Together forever."

"I'll go with you, Ken. I—I've missed you, too. But I'll need to pack. I can't leave right this minute."

"Did you miss me?" A shadow passed over his face. "You didn't answer my letter, so I went to see you. You had a man living with you, Claire. You must remember it this time."

"My cousin." She tried to squirm out from behind Jacob. He leaned back, pinning her so firmly against the car that she could scarcely breathe. She couldn't see around him—only the dark sleeve of Ken's suit, a glimpse of his shoulder. The gun in his hand. "You remember my cousin Danny, don't you?"

"He took advantage of you." Ken spoke with the eerie, mild displeasure she remembered too well. The hand holding the gun dipped slightly. Not enough. "You shouldn't have let him do that, but I forgave you. Again. I know you don't mean to hurt me, but now you're with someone else. He's standing there between us, and that's wrong. I can't let others come between us. You know that." The gun barrel lifted and steadied. "I'll shoot him if he doesn't move."

"You can shoot me," Jacob said, his voice deep and steady. "But you might want to think about it first. That's a .357 in your hand."

"It is?" Ken was curious, polite. "I don't know a lot about guns. Fortunately you don't have to know much to buy one. Or to use it."

"A bullet from that gun would go right though me and hurt Claire. You don't want to hurt Claire."

Ken's voice lost none of its certainty. "We have to be together. Together forever…in paradise."

Together in death. Claire heard the words as clearly as if he'd spoken them. He'd come to kill her and himself—and if Jacob didn't move, Ken would kill him, too. Suddenly she was very cold, and very calm. She didn't know if she could save herself, but somehow she had to save Jacob.

Who was damnably determined to shield her with his body. "If you kill me," he said in the same reasonable voice she'd heard him use when dealing with a reluctant stockholder, "I'll be in paradise along with you and Claire. That's not what you want."

"No. No, I don't know where you'll go, but you won't be with us. Claire and I are fated to be one, but she can't handle the temptations on this earthly plane.'' Ken sounded sad—not angry, not grieving or insane. Just sad. ''She doesn't mean to hurt me. She's just too beautiful. Every man who sees her wants her, and she can't help herself. So I have to help her.''

''I don't think shooting her will help her.''

Ken's voice was firmer now. Condescending. ''Of course you don't. I can't expect you to grasp the nature of our bond. It's unfortunate that your lack of understanding is going to kill you.''

She saw Ken's arm lift. And she glimpsed, behind him, a blur of motion—Jackie running flat-out, her long legs flinging her forward in a leap that belonged in the record books.

Jackie crashed into Ken's back, jerking his arm up as they fell. The gun went off—pointed straight up at the sky.

The sky was smoggy with dusk by the time they pulled up in front of Jacob's house. He didn't want to drive around back to the garage, didn't want to spend the few extra minutes that would take. He wanted Claire inside, in his home. Safe. The need was primal and undeniable, however little sense it made. Lawrence was locked away again.

But it had been close. So close. He'd nearly lost her. If Jackie Muldrow hadn't had a hunch, hadn't trusted it... she'd had a feeling, she'd told them later. Just a feeling. Or maybe it had been pure frustration when none of her leads panned out that had sent her to the hospital to talk to Danny again, see if he'd remembered anything more.

If she hadn't...

He didn't want to think about that.

Jacob had seen the sergeant. With his back pressed up against Claire, protecting her the only way he could, he'd glimpsed her moving between the parked cars. Until then, he'd thought only chance was to throw himself at Lawrence and hope Claire escaped. Once he'd seen the cop, though, he'd tried to stall. To keep the man talking—until someone else could save Claire.

Jacob scowled and slammed the car door behind him. It didn't help.

"God." Claire stood next to the car, both hands threaded in her hair, her head tilted back. The air was dead quiet, not a breath of a breeze. And cold. Winter had finally arrived, blown in on the tail of the storm last night. "I can hardly believe it's really over."

He looked at the smooth arch of her throat. His own throat felt raw.

It's over. She meant her fear, the whole ugly situation with Lawrence. Jacob knew that. She didn't mean that *they* were over.

But Claire didn't need him now.

Not that he'd been much good when she had needed him. "He'll be put where he belongs this time. Your friend will see to that—just like she took care of everything else."

She dropped her hands and looked at him. Then came to him, not speaking until she stood a heartbeat away. "What's wrong?"

"Nothing. We should go in." But he didn't move. So close, he had come so close to losing her.

"Something's wrong. You look like an explosion about to happen."

He managed a grim twitch of his lips that he hoped could pass for a smile. "It's been an eventful day."

"And you haven't held me since nearly squeezing the life out of me while Jackie was clamping the handcuffs on Ken." She moved a whisper closer, reaching up to touch his cheek. "What is it, Jacob?"

The feelings inside him wound a hard notch tighter. "If

your friend hadn't come when she did…dammit, Claire, I wasn't much use. I promised to protect you, but when it came time for a rescue, your friend did the job.''

Her eyes widened. ''You shielded me with your body. Which, by the way, makes me furious every time I think about it. Just what more do you think you were supposed to do?''

''Something! I should have done something, anything.'' He dragged a hand through his hair. ''I never want to be as helpless again as I was then, standing there, waiting for him to put a bullet in you—''

''In *you*, you idiot!'' Her fingers dug into his shoulders as if she wanted to shake him. ''Do you have any idea what that did to me?''

Fear, past and present, whipped higher. Fury threatened to break through—fury at himself, at Lawrence, at the system that hadn't kept Lawrence penned up. And at her, for being the center of the emotions building, cyclone strong, inside him.

A muscle jumped in his cheek. His hands were careful when they removed hers from his shoulders. ''Claire. I'm not *safe* right now. You don't want to be touching me. I need time to calm down.''

She gave him a quick, impatient frown. And stretched up on tiptoe to crush her mouth against his.

Claire felt the quiver run through Jacob when she leaned against him, body to body, standing on tiptoe so she could make the fit as complete as possible. She pressed herself— mouth, body and heart—against him, willing the stupid man to *know* she was safe with him.

Every bit as safe as she wanted to be.

He froze. It lasted one quick spit of a second, then his arms snapped around her, holding her desperation-tight. Tight enough to steal her breath, and send her soaring.

This wasn't the careful man she'd known. This man hungered so fiercely he lifted her off her feet, the throb of his erection setting up an answering throb between her legs. He groaned and swept a hand over her back, squeezing her buttocks, pulling her tighter against him. His tongue plunged inside her mouth.

Inside. Yes, she needed him inside her, filling her, making her whole—but they were outside. Standing on the cold cement of his driveway, three steps from his car. On the wrong side of his front door.

She tore her mouth from his. "Jacob…"

Her hands, clenched in his hair, may have given him the idea she wanted his mouth elsewhere. On her cheek, her throat, trailing heat down the neckline of her jacket. The muscles in his arms bunched, and he lifted her higher, nuzzling at the collar of her jacket. In another second, he'd have it pushed aside and be blazing a trail across her breast.

She threw back her head and laughed with sheer exhilaration. "Jacob," she tried again, this time tugging at his hair to get his attention. "We're in your driveway."

He lifted his eyes. For a second his eyes were blind, unfocused—then filled with horror. "God, I'm sorry. I'm sorry, I didn't mean—" He let go of her so quickly she landed back on her feet with a thump.

"Don't." She curved her arms around his waist in a quick hug. "Don't apologize. I want you wild, to match the wildness in me. I need that. But maybe we should go inside first?" She smiled wickedly and leaned back so she could drift the tips of her breasts across his chest.

His breath hitched. Then, slowly, he smiled back. Twice as wickedly.

They made it inside, but they didn't make it to his bed. Not right away. Jacob had called Cosmo from the hospital, giving him the bare bones of the tale, and he and Ada were waiting for them.

Claire understood. These people loved Jacob, too, in their different ways. They, too, needed to confirm with their senses that he was alive and whole. Ada fussed at him and dragged them both to the kitchen to feed them. Cosmo trailed after them, waving his arms in sweeping gestures, demanding details and wishing loudly he had been there.

But eventually, after she'd pushed some food around on her plate and answered a few hundred questions, Claire decided that enough was enough. She yawned once, then again.

Her yawns didn't fool anyone. Ada smirked. Cosmo patted her shoulder and suggested oh-so-innocently that she needed some extra B-complex vitamins—for energy. And Jacob frowned. "Claire, you're falling asleep sitting up. You've had a rough day. You'd better go to bed."

It was eight o'clock. Did the fool man really think she wanted to sleep? Just to make sure he got the point, she pushed her chair back, stood, and smiled at him. "You still haven't shown me where to put my things. I'm not going to move all my clothes into your closet tonight, but I'll need a few odds and ends with me."

Maybe his slow blink meant she'd surprised him. Maybe—judging by the sudden heat in his eyes—it meant he needed a moment to gather his control before he grabbed her and dragged her upstairs.

She was hoping for the latter.

Jacob helped her pack. He was in an odd, playful mood, teasing her about the amount of cosmetics and cleansers she considered essential, insisting on selecting her night-gown himself. His eyes were bright, more alive than she'd even seen them. He didn't touch her.

She knew why. There was a bed in this room. Anticipation and heat coiled in her belly, a lazy serpent awaiting the slightest provocation to strike. If Jacob had touched her even once, however lightly, they would never have made it upstairs, to his room. His bed.

She wanted to be in his bed.

He stayed in the same playful mood all the way up the stairs—then, at the top, he scooped her up in his arms.

"Hey!" She grabbed his neck and hung on. "What are you doing?"

"Being romantic. I would have carried you all the way, but I wasn't sure I could make it up all those stairs."

"That's romantic—hinting that I weigh a ton?"

He gave her one of those slow, sexy smiles, looking very sure of himself. Or maybe of her. "You don't need me to tell you how beautiful you are. You've got a mirror for that."

She drew her fingers along the back of his neck. "A woman always needs to know she's beautiful to—to the man she's about to give herself to." *The man I love.* Her heart beat faster. How would he have reacted if she had said that?

His eyes darkened. He dipped his head to kiss her, slowly, lingeringly. He was still kissing her when he shoved his door open—and closed it behind them.

Jacob seemed to have in mind a gradual wooing of her senses. She didn't. She wanted him to explode with her the way he nearly had out in the driveway. She wanted straining limbs, shivering flesh and both of them wild. "Let's speed things up," she whispered, kissing his neck.

His hands tightened at her waist. "How fast?"

"Fast enough to wipe everything else out."

He swept her up in his arms, tossed her on the bed—and came down on it with her, grinning. Oh, that grin—it transformed him. For a moment he was boyish—purely, simply, happy. Then he kissed her again, and he was all man. Hot, hungry, impatient man.

But still controlled. Even when his hands shook, he didn't lose himself. She could feel him holding back, and it drove her crazy. She wrapped her hand around him and he shuddered—and clasped both her hands in his, drawing them over her head, then bent to drive her insane with his mouth.

Claire knew Jacob needed his control. She valued it, too, because it was part of him, part of the strength and integrity that made him who he was. But damned if she would tolerate it in bed. The second his hand relaxed its grip she tugged hers free, twisted, and trailed kisses down his chest, his stomach…and below. She got her mouth on him—one long, slow lick of her tongue. And she got her explosion.

He bucked. And grabbed her, his fingers digging into her hips, and rolled her onto her back. Thrust her legs wide, and thrust himself inside.

She climaxed on the second stroke in a breath-stealing punch that crashed, then dimmed—then ripened once more, his body calling hotly to hers until she was sobbing, clawing his back and calling his name.

He cried out her name, too, as he slammed into her one last time—and sent her tripping and falling, falling where there was nothing, and no one, but him. Only him.

Eons later, her breathing had slowed and her mind had mostly returned. He still lay on top of her, heavy and limp, infinitely welcome.

"You decided to kill me?" he murmured next to her ear, then gathered her close and shifted onto his side. "Funny. I didn't know we'd still sweat in the afterlife." He pressed one drowsy kiss on her mouth. "I love you, Claire."

And she went stiff. Silent. And scared.

He didn't say anything more. He didn't stiffen the way

she had, but he pulled away into the same dreadful silence. After a long moment, he kissed her on the cheek. Then he rolled over—onto his back, then his side. Putting his back to her.

Tears stung her eyes. *Why?* she demanded of herself, but there was no answer, only an oily darkness churning inside her that she couldn't name or dismiss.

After a moment she forced herself to roll onto her side, to put her arm around him and snuggle close. It helped, a little. At least he didn't push her away. "Jacob?" Her voice quivered from the effort to hold back the tears.

"Go to sleep, Claire."

His voice was quiet, unemotional. But the very lack of emotion told her what she already knew. She'd hurt him terribly.

And she didn't know why.

Twelve

"No, not the bank," Jacob said, drumming his fingers on his desk. "I'll have to obtain a private loan. A balloon note, I think, due in a year."

Claire looked up, surprised. They'd been discussing his options, how to amend the joint venture agreement with Murchison out of the picture and where to get the two million. "There's no reason to delay repayment that long. It increases the amount of interest you'll owe. And why not a bank?"

His fingers stopped. His eyes were cool, impatient. "I believe I'm aware of the basics of financing. The interest won't be ruinous."

"No, just unnecessary. It won't take that long to dissolve the trust—unless there's some question about that? You said Luke had already married. If Michael is having some trouble finding someone—"

"Michael's prenuptial agreement is in the safe. He will do what he has to."

The world went flat and gray. "Then it isn't Luke's and Michael's marriages you're concerned about."

"No." He paused. "I think it would be best if we postponed our wedding."

Claire looked away, trying to hide the staggering hit of pain. Maybe she deserved it, but that didn't help. It didn't help at all.

Jacob had been gone when she woke up that morning. She'd tried to find him before breakfast and again after breakfast, but he'd left the house. An hour ago he'd returned and starting discussing business.

It took her a moment, but she pulled herself together. "I don't want to put it off. Jacob, about last night—"

"I've rushed you. I promised you at least a month, then pushed you into marrying in less than a week. That was unfair. We'll wait." He riffled through the pages of a report. "Where's Benson's profit-loss summary?"

"Page ten, I think. How long…" She had to stop and swallow. "How long do you want to wait? My mother will need to change her reservations."

"I don't know." His voice was crisp. He wouldn't look at her. "Why don't we wait and see? I'm not going to rush you, Claire. Now, about Benson—it looks as if he might have enough free to increase his investment in the deal. Give him a call after you talk to my lawyer about amending the agreement. I'll see who would like to loan me two million dollars, give or take a few hundred thousand."

"You sure you don't want some of this rocky road?" Jackie asked.

Claire continued to pace the length of her friend's living

room—all fourteen jumbled, Technicolor feet of it. "I can't eat."

"Things have to be pretty bad when rocky road ice cream won't help." Jackie's words were flippant, but her eyes were luminous with sympathy. "I might have a beer in the fridge if you'd rather have that."

"No, thanks."

"You want to stop moving long enough to tell me what's wrong?"

"Me." Claire did stop. "*I'm* what's wrong, Jackie, and I don't understand." She shoved her hair back from her face. "Dammit, I ought to chop this mess off. It drives me crazy sometimes."

"When you start talking about butchering your hair, I know you've got troubles. Come on." She rimmed her almost-empty bowl with the spoon, then licked the last drops from the spoon. "Sit down here and tell me about it."

Claire plopped onto the sofa beside her friend. "I'm losing my mind."

"Well, that's a start. Can you be more specific? Obsession, mania, hallucinations?"

She gave a reluctant chuckle. "Nothing quite that dramatic. I just…I hurt Jacob. I hurt myself, too, and I don't know why." Jackie didn't say a word. Claire looked at her. "Is this how you get suspects to talk? Just look at them with that wise, knowing expression, say nothing and wait for them to spill their guts?"

"Damn right. It works, too."

"It does, doesn't it?" Claire sighed. "Three nights ago, Jacob told me he loved me. And I froze up like an eighty-year-old virgin on her wedding night."

"Hmm." Jackie set her bowl on the floor beside her. "You're not sure if you love him back?"

"I love him." The certainty was there, bright and strong as ever. "I've had some doubts about rushing into marriage this way, but that's because it all happened so fast. I didn't know if I could get him to love me back. Then, when he said it—" She shoved to her feet and started pacing again. "I freaked out. Quietly, without saying a word…but he knew."

"So what did he say?"

"That he wants to postpone the wedding. Indefinitely." She'd tried to talk to him, but maybe she hadn't tried very hard. He'd been pleasant, kind, and implacably distant. And she didn't know what she would tell him if she did make him listen. That she loved him, but it scared her to hear he loved her back? That didn't make any sense.

"So…" Jackie said after a moment's silence. "Is he still sleeping with you?"

"Jackie!"

"If he isn't, you've got a real problem. If he is, then things can't be too bad."

"They're not good." Claire had moved her things into his room. She slept there every night—and every night he made love to her. Silently. In complete control of himself.

"Well, whether or not you're still making the beast with two humps, half of this problem is his. He doesn't seem to be doing much to fix it, either."

She sighed. "I don't blame him." Tears threatened for the ninety-ninth time in the past three days. "He needs someone he can count on. He needs permanence. That's why he loves that old house so much, because it's always been there. He can count on it, like he counts on Ada. I let him down in the worst possible way."

"Oh, come on. Not the worst. You didn't cheat on him, lie to him, hit him over the head with a baseball bat."

"You don't understand." For once, she had little patience with Jackie's irreverent humor. "Jacob needs—"

"Never mind what Jacob needs. I'd say you've got some needs you haven't looked at, or you wouldn't be clouding up and threatening to storm all over my living room."

"I am not crying." Yet. Her feet drifted to a stop. "I just don't understand why I reacted that way. I don't know how to make things right when I don't understand what's wrong with me!"

"Scared you, did he?" Jackie's voice was gentle. "Kind of overwhelming to suddenly get everything you ever wanted. Especially if you aren't sure you deserve it. Someone might notice, and take it away again."

"I'm not that messed up."

"Oh, sugar." Jackie laughed. "We are *all* that messed up, one way or another. Your big thing is atonement."

Her eyebrows lifted in a weak pass at humor. "You have something against sackcloth and ashes? I'll admit I did try them on for a while, right after Ken's trial. But I'm over that. I had therapy, remember? I don't blame myself for Ken's madness."

"No, you blame yourself for loving him in the first place. Flunked that one, didn't you?" Jackie uncoiled a mile or two of legs and stood. "Fact is, Ken was just another bump along the same road you've been on for years—blaming yourself for not loving people enough, or loving the wrong people, or doing it the wrong way." She snorted. "As if you were trying to pass Love 101."

"I don't do that."

"Yes, sugar, you do." Jackie's eyes were sympathetic, but she didn't let up one bit. "Ever since you came dragging back from California with your tail between your legs when you were sixteen, you've been trying to make it up to everyone. To prove you were worthy of love. You were convinced you'd ruined your cousin's life, your life, you mom's life, your stepdad's…shoot, if I'd screwed up and married Roger when he asked me back then, you probably would have blamed yourself for that, too.''

For a moment Claire was speechless. ''I had no idea you saw me that way.'' It hurt.

''You're human, Claire, just like the rest of us. And your mistakes aren't quite as big and important as you think they are. Even this one you just made, with Jacob.''

Claire rubbed her forehead. She wanted to push away everything Jackie had said, deny it, walk away, just walk right out the door—but some of it was sticking. As if it belonged to her. ''All this good advice is giving me a headache.''

Jackie grinned. ''Ice cream is great for headaches.''

Claire's laugh wasn't steady, but it was genuine. ''You just want an excuse to have another bowl.''

''Couldn't let you eat alone, could I? Come on.'' She gave Claire a quick, one-armed hug. ''Let's pig out. Then we can figure out how you're going to make it up to Jacob for being human.''

Jacob stood by the window and sipped at his drink—Irish whiskey, not Scotch. No rain had fallen for days, and the sky was a vast, brilliant blue. The color of childhood, to Jacob. Of solitude and freedom.

He'd never thought of freedom as lonely before.

He was doing the right thing, he told himself. At least, he was doing the only thing he knew to do, and it wasn't totally wrong. He knew that much, because she hadn't left him.

Though she wasn't here now. She'd asked for the afternoon off so she could go see her friend. But she would be back. She slept in his bed every night, and she gave herself to him with a sweet warmth he craved more each time he held her.

He could make it work...as long as he didn't say he loved her.

The pain was strong and livid. He couldn't seem to grow used to it, to let the hurt scab over and fade.

Impatient, Jacob turned away from the window. Blurting out his feelings that way had been stupid. He hadn't known he was going to do it. He hadn't—until he heard himself say the words—known that he loved her. The truth had floated up so naturally, he'd had no defense against it.

He hadn't been thinking of defenses.

He reminded himself that Claire had heard those same words from another man that day. A man who'd tried to kill her. Jacob didn't exactly sympathize with the poor bastard, but he understood Lawrence's need to keep Claire. He shared it.

The sound of the front door opening, then shutting, was muted back here in his office. But he heard it, and his heartbeat picked up.

She was back. Because he needed to be sure he wouldn't grab her the moment she walked in the office, he turned to the window. He was standing with his back to the door when it opened.

"You don't drink during office hours."

Her voice, husky and low, sent a thrill up his spine. He gave himself a moment to control that by sipping at his drink. "I decided to knock off early today. Did you enjoy your visit?"

"It was...productive. There's something I'd like to show you, if you'd turn around."

Slowly, he did.

Her hair was mussed, from wind or her own restless fingers. She'd dressed casually to go see her friend; denim hugged her legs and hips like an old, intimate friend. Her sweater was a soft, faded blue with white buttons down the front. He couldn't keep from soaking up the sight of her, but he could and did keep his reaction from showing.

At first. He frowned. "You're not wearing a bra."

"I had to take it off." Her chin tilted up. "Are you going to ask me why?"

"I'll admit to some curiosity," he said dryly.

"I'll show you." Her fingers went to the first button on her sweater.

"Claire." His mouth went dry and his pulse began to hammer. "This isn't the time or place."

"Why not?" Another button. "Because you and I both find it a little too easy to blot our problems out with passion? Because we have trouble talking about what really matters?"

"You don't seem to be talking." He couldn't take his eyes away from the slow progress of that hand. Three buttons were undone, and the sweater gapped open, revealing the smooth, pale inner slopes of her breasts. His mouth went dry.

"I'm not sure words would be enough, after I rejected the words you gave me." Her voice scraped up against emotions still raw in him. And, he thought, in her. "That's why I need to show you how I feel."

She wanted him. It should have been enough. It wasn't. His voice came out harsh. "You were frightened."

"Yes, though how you knew that when I was so confused…" The last button seemed stubborn, or maybe her fingers were shaking. "I'm sorry, Jacob." She took a deep breath, and opened her sweater.

Shock widened his eyes, coarsened his voice. "Claire, there's a tattoo on your breast."

"Yes." Her eyes were huge and vulnerable. And she strode towards him with the confidence of an empress, bare-breasted and magnificent.

He couldn't take his eyes from her breasts. Her left breast, to be precise, about an inch and a half from her nipple. Drawn there in a warm, rosy red was the outline of a heart, the sort seen on children's valentines. A stick drawing, with an arrow piercing it.

Inside the heart were words: *Claire loves Jacob.*

He lifted stunned eyes to her face.

Tears blurred her eyes, but didn't fall. "Tattoos are permanent, Jacob. They're forever, or as close to it as we can get. And I—I wanted to show you that I know you don't just want the outside of me, the pretty parts. You care about what's inside, too, and I don't have to be perfect for you. I can be—" Her breath hitched. "A little wild, a little dumb. Impulsive. And imperfect. And it will still be okay." She stopped. "Won't it?"

The feelings bursting inside him were too new, too vibrant for words. He lifted a hand to touch her face—but his fingers went to her breast instead. Lightly, lightly, he felt the outline of that outrageous, courageous, permanent heart.

She winced. "It's a little sore. They, ah, they just did it."

"You went to a tattoo parlor." A grin was trying to break out.

"With Jackie. I'd like to claim this was her idea, but I guess part of me is still fifteen and crazy." Her grin appeared, and wobbled. "This time they didn't ask for my ID."

"You got a tattoo on your breast." If he said the words clearly enough, he might be able to tuck them down deep inside and keep them—and all that they meant. "To prove to me that you love me."

She nodded, and his bright, bold, beautiful Claire looked shy standing there with her breasts bare in the afternoon sunlight. "It isn't too late, is it? Jacob, tell me it—"

He laughed. Laughed and grabbed her and spun them both in a quick, dizzy circle. "You *are* crazy, you know that?"

"I hope you mean good-crazy, not lock-me-away nuts." Her hands were on his shoulders, the light shining in her face brighter than that pouring through the window.

"A very good way." He pressed a kiss to her mouth. Another. "A very, very good way. I was afraid I'd pushed you too hard, that I reminded you of Lawrence. I wanted to keep you so much. Claire."

"You're nothing like Ken. And love isn't obsession. I've finally figured that out."

He gathered his courage and asked, "What do you think of a Christmas wedding? I don't want to wait too long. And it has nothing to do with Tristar, or the trust."

"I think it would be perfect." She kissed him once, lightly. Again, more firmly. "Absolutely perfect."

Everything came together at once, so strong he could only crush her to him, burying his face in her hair. "Claire. You love me."

He felt her head nod against his shoulder. "I do. It's pretty big and scary, isn't it?"

"Yes." He stroked her hair. "The words scared me, too. I wouldn't use them if they didn't mean forever, but I wasn't sure…I'm thirty-six and I've never been in love. I thought I might be like my father. I didn't want to make his mistakes.''

"Jacob.'' She leaned back in his arms and touched his face. "You're not like your father. You take after Ada.''

"But she isn't—Ada is family, but there's no blood relationship.''

Her smile was tender. "She's been your mother in the important ways. She's a natural caretaker, like you are. So you modeled yourself after her—gruff and unsentimental, with a wicked sense of humor.''

He felt unsettled. "You liked Ada right away.''

"Yes.'' Claire laughed softly. "Although, when you were telling me how you'd deceived her for her own good, I felt a little jealous. That's when I knew how far gone I was. Because I actually wished you'd lie to me, too, someday. You never lie, but you loved Ada enough to sacrifice even that for her sake.''

He kissed her gently. "I love you, too.'' More. Brighter, stronger, better than he'd thought was possible.

"I know.'' She sighed and settled closer against him. "And I wanted you to love me, but I thought I had to do everything right, that I needed to earn that love. I was so scared of doing the wrong thing…and then I did. I thought I'd ruined everything.''

"You didn't mess up. I did. I should have realized those words might scare you, after what happened with Lawrence…'' His arms tightened involuntarily.

She flinched.

Immediately he loosened his hold. "You're sore.''

"Tender,'' she corrected wryly. "It will pass.''

"I could kiss it and make it better.''

"Not for another day or so. I'm, ah, supposed to keep it dry for a while."

Regret pinched lightly at having to wait to kiss that very special mark, but he thought of all the time—the days, the years—they would have when he could kiss her there, and elsewhere. Years to spend treasuring her. He snuggled her close again. "I must have done something right, but damned if I know what it was. I never did figure out what you needed, what I could give you."

"Jacob." She caught his face in her hands, and smiled. "That's the easiest answer of all. You. You're what I needed all along."

* * * * *

How did Luke end up married to Maggie?
Find out next month in LUKE'S PROMISE.
Only from Eileen Wilks—and Silhouette Desire!

CALL THE ONES YOU LOVE OVER THE HOLIDAYS!

Save $25 off future book purchases when you buy any four Harlequin® or Silhouette® books in October, November and December 2001,

PLUS

receive a phone card good for 15 minutes of long-distance calls to anyone you want in North America!

WHAT AN INCREDIBLE DEAL!

Just fill out this form and attach 4 proofs of purchase (cash register receipts) from October, November and December 2001 books, and Harlequin Books will send you a coupon booklet worth a total savings of $25 off future purchases of Harlequin® and Silhouette® books, AND a 15-minute phone card to call the ones you love, anywhere in North America.

Please send this form, along with your cash register receipts
as proofs of purchase, to:
In the USA: Harlequin Books, P.O. Box 9057, Buffalo, NY 14269-9057
In Canada: Harlequin Books, P.O. Box 622, Fort Erie, Ontario L2A 5X3
Cash register receipts must be dated no later than December 31, 2001.
Limit of 1 coupon booklet and phone card per household.
Please allow 4-6 weeks for delivery.

I accept your offer! Please send me my coupon booklet and a 15-minute phone card:

Name: _____

Address: _____ City: _____

State/Prov.: _____ Zip/Postal Code: _____

Account Number (if available): _____

---

097 KJB DAGL
PHQ4012

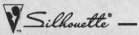

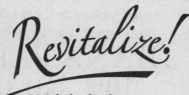

Silhouette Books cordially invites you to come
on down to Jacobsville, Texas, for

DIANA PALMER's
LONG, TALL TEXAN
Weddings

(On sale November 2001)

The LONG, TALL TEXANS series from international
bestselling author Diana Palmer is cherished around the
world. Now three sensuous, charming love stories from
this blockbuster series—*Coltrain's Proposal, Beloved* and
"Paper Husband"—are available in one special volume!

*As free as wild mustangs, Jeb, Simon and Hank vowed
never to submit to the reins of marriage. Until, of course,
a certain trio of provocative beauties tempt these Lone Star
lovers off the range…and into a tender, timeless embrace!*

You won't want to miss
LONG, TALL TEXAN WEDDINGS
by Diana Palmer, featuring two
full-length novels and one short story!

Available only from Silhouette Books at your favorite retail outlet.

Where love comes alive™

Visit Silhouette at www.eHarlequin.com

PSLTTW